WINDS OF HOPE

ALSO BY THE AUTHOR

FICTION BY REBECCA CAREY LYLES

Kate Neilson Series

Winds of Wyoming (Book One)

Winds of Freedom (Book Two)

Winds of Change (Book Three)

———————

Short Stories

Passageways: A Short Story Collection

———————

NONFICTION BY BECKY LYLES

*It's a God Thing! Inspiring Stories of
Life-Changing Friendships*

*On a Wing and a Prayer: Stories from
Freedom Fellowship, a Prison Ministry*

———————

Prequel to the Kate Neilson Series

WINDS OF

HOPE

REBECCA CAREY LYLES

PERPEDIT ✔ PUBLISHING, INK

Perpedit Publishing, Ink
PO Box 190246
Boise, Idaho 83719

http://www.perpedit.com

First eBook Edition: 2017
First Paperback Edition: 2017
ISBN: 13: 978-0-9894624-6-4 (eBook)
ISBN: 13: 978-0-9894624-7-1 (Paperback)

Cover design by Ken Koeberlein of Koeber Designs

Published in the United States of America
Perpedit Publishing, Ink

DEDICATION

This book is dedicated to the memory of my homesteading grandparents, the Careys and the Chisholms, who risked all to establish a future for their children on the windy Wyoming prairie, where meadowlarks sing, wheat grows tall, and the deer and the antelope play.

"I'm fortunate to live in Wyoming, one of the most beautiful,
pristine places in the world."
John Barrasso, Wyoming Senator

Twilight silently, softly falls,
Touching valley and grove with misty wand,
Kissing the sky goodnight at the west;
From far-off peaks of the mountain-land.
All nature slumbers in perfect rest,
Sweet sleep the earth enfolds.

Night lures to soft Elysian dreams,
And far and wide dominion holds;
No sound invades save distant wail
Of coyote from the upland steep,
Or gentle tinkle of a brook
In rocky butte or cañon deep.

And here in this Sweet-Water vale,
How pleasant the passing years should flow;
A vale engirdled by Rocky Peak,
A grand, majestic show!

Excerpt taken from *The Scenery & Game of Wyoming Territory*
by Isaac McLellan (1806-1899)

"In Wyoming, the beauty of our mountains is matched only by the
grit of our people."
Liz Cheney, Wyoming Congresswoman

"It's kind of a Wyoming thing to push the whole 'Wild West'
routine to its limits."
From *Glass Girl* by Laura Anderson Kurk

KATE

THE PRISON GATE CLANGED SHUT behind Kate Neilson, the sound as loud and harsh in her ears as coupling train cars. She'd heard that clatter of metal against metal hundreds of times during her five years of incarceration. Yet with each slam, her stomach lurched and her shoulders jerked. Try as she might to steel herself against the jarring crash, she couldn't help but react like a startled bird.

For the first time, Kate stood on the visitor side of the barred gate that separated the reception area from the wide fluorescent-lit hallway leading to the cellblocks. She still had to walk out the front door of the building and through a gate in the fence that surrounded Patterson State Penitentiary. But she'd crossed the final interior barrier.

The female correctional officer who escorted her, Officer Arledge, paused and spoke into the radio clipped to her gray shirt, notifying the control desk of their location. Kate clutched the plastic sack that held the meager possessions she'd accumulated during her time at Patterson and took a steadying breath. The room smelled vaguely familiar.

Floor wax. That's what it was. The smooth surface at her feet was so highly polished it reflected the ceiling lights. On the other side of the bars, the gray concrete floors were mopped by inmates but never waxed.

She could have turned for one last glimpse through the gate. After all, the building housed the culture that had transformed her from a lost-and-lonely Pittsburgh street tramp into a college graduate with a marketing degree. Instead, she focused on the double glass doors at the other end of the room, doors that led to freedom and to her future.

Unlike the muted light that filtered from the glass blocks imbedded in her cell wall, sunshine streamed through the doors, illuminating columns of dust motes. But as much as she itched to dart across the room and charge outside, she had one more hurdle to clear. Between her and liberty stood a reception desk staffed by two male COs seated before computer monitors.

She had a side view of the men. Like the female officer, they wore light gray shirts, dark gray pants and black duty belts. Loops and pouches attached to the belts held flashlights, pepper spray, eye protection, handcuffs, handcuff keys and more—but no guns. Kate couldn't see their feet, but she'd never seen COs wear anything but black work boots identical to what the officer beside her had on her feet.

Arledge motioned her toward the desk. "The last phase of your checkout is here."

Earlier that morning, just before she left her unit, Kate had been strip-searched. She'd endured the humiliating contraband hunt on more occasions than she cared to remember, and she hoped to never again hear, "Strip,

Neilson." But right now, she would comply with everything the COs asked of her—whatever it took to walk out those doors today.

At the desk, Arledge stated Kate's last name and inmate number. One of the men said, "I already have your file pulled up, Ms. Neilson."

Kate smiled for the first time since she'd started the nerve-racking trek from the far side of the massive compound. Whether intentional or not, he'd called her *Ms. Neilson*, not just *Neilson* or her number.

The printer behind the man whirred to life and spit out two sheets of paper, one after the other. He pulled them from the tray. "We have two final forms for you to sign." Sliding one of the papers onto the counter, he said, "This one says we returned all the items you had with you when you were admitted."

Kate pressed her lips together. *Admitted* suggested she'd been checked into a hospital for short-term care, not into a prison for five mind-numbing years of incarceration. She kept her thoughts to herself and placed the bag she'd carried across the complex on the counter.

The other officer produced a sealed plastic pouch from beneath the desk. The clear pocket on the front had also been sealed. Inside was the card Kate filled out when she first entered the facility. He pulled scissors from a drawer, cut the bag and the pocket open, and shook out the contents.

A lacy red thong landed on top of the pile. The corner of his mouth twitched and he glanced at the other male officer before giving her instructions. "Check the contents against the card. If everything is there, sign the form." He handed her a pen.

Kate ignored his smirk and pushed aside the underwear, along with the skimpy tank top and threadbare cutoff shorts she'd been wearing when she was arrested. The clothing still held a hint of the perfume she favored back then. She checked off the items. No bra was listed because she hadn't worn one that night—she never wore one when she worked the streets.

The collection was small. She was glad to see her watch, a birthday gift from her Great-Aunt Mary, but the screen was blank. Probably needed a new battery. She picked up her driver's license, saw that it had expired, and made a mental note to stop by the DMV to pick up a manual.

She would have to take the driver's test again to get a valid license so she could drive to Wyoming. Her stomach jumped again, but this was a happy jolt because she'd been accepted for a marketing internship at a guest ranch. Her girlhood dream of visiting a Wyoming ranch was about to come true.

Worn black sandals, a comb, lip gloss, two condoms and a mascara tube were the only other items on the counter. The money she'd had in her pocket had been deposited into her commissary account. Kate checked the final box. "Everything's here." She took a moment to read the form before she signed it.

"Place your possessions in the bag," Arledge said, "and take it to the restroom over there. After you change into street clothes, return the bag, shoes, socks and uniform here. You may keep the underwear."

Kate started to go, but Arledge stopped her. "Leave your ID."

Kate pulled the lanyard over her head and around her long hair. The ID tag dangling from the end weighed no more than a credit card, yet she felt as though a boulder lifted from her shoulders. To rid herself of prison ID meant she really was on her way out of Patterson.

The restroom looked nothing like the other bathrooms in the prison and smelled a whole lot better. Kate was about to enter a stall, when she glimpsed herself in the bright, clean mirror. Caught off-guard, she stopped and stared. She hadn't seen a clear reflection in years. The scuffed stainless-steel rectangles that served as mirrors in the inmate bathrooms blurred every image.

She squinted. *So that's what prison food does to a person.* She appeared older and heavier, her dark hair and dark eyes had dulled, and her face was... She grimaced. Pasty, puffy, haggard...guarded.

Sighing, she turned away. Time to make some changes. She'd walked the track around the yard almost every day of her incarceration. But apparently fifteen minutes twice a day wasn't enough exercise *or* sunshine.

Kate tossed the thong into the trash receptacle, slipped off the shoes, socks and elastic-waist orange pants, and pulled the orange shirt over her head. She folded the clothes and set them aside. Never, *never* again would she wear orange. She pulled on the tank top and then the shorts, which she managed to zip and button only after she sucked in her stomach.

Stepping into the sandals, she thanked God she hadn't been released in winter. Her clothes barely covered her. She was also grateful she didn't have to walk out of prison braless and embarrass Aunt Mary. Even so, she would dump the prison undergarments the moment she unboxed her clothes, which were stored in her aunt's attic, last she knew. And she'd drop the extra weight. In the meantime, she hoped she'd fit into at least a few things.

Kate fastened the watch onto her wrist and stuffed the other items into her skintight pockets before she returned to the reception desk. After years of wearing loose prison uniforms, she felt like a sausage in the close-fitting clothes. Averting her gaze from the male officers' appreciative glances, she laid the bag and prison garb on the counter. "Anything else?"

The CO with the paperwork handed her a check for her commissary balance and had her sign a form stating that the prison returned the correct amount to her.

Kate thanked him, folded the check and shoved it into a back pocket. The digital clock on the wall behind the reception desk flashed eight-eleven in large red numerals. One of Aunt Mary's friends from church, Gertie Mae Spaulding, was driving her to the prison. They'd been advised to arrive by eight-thirty.

"I'll accompany you to the entrance," Arledge said. She turned to the men. "Please let the front gate know we're coming."

The two gave each other side glances, as if they didn't care to take orders from a woman. Kate had seen similar standoffs between other female COs and the male COs who outnumbered them two to one. She glanced at the clock and then back at Arledge.

The woman eyed the men until one of them reached for the phone. Apparently satisfied he'd do what she asked, she strode toward the glass doors, her sturdy body outlined by sunshine. She opened one and motioned Kate through.

The dazzling sunlight blinded Kate. She sneezed and nearly ran into Officer Strunk, an obnoxious man the women in her unit had nicknamed "Skunk" his first day on the job.

Strunk inspected her from head to toe and up again. "So, they're letting you out, Neilson." With an arrogant rise of his eyebrows, he added, "Going back to your old occupation?"

She didn't respond.

"I'll give you a month." He sneered. "By then you'll be working the streets again, 'cause we all know you can't make it in the real world. Hill District, right?"

Kate, who was well-practiced at maintaining a deadpan demeanor, hoped he couldn't see her inward cringe.

Arledge glared at him. "One of these days…" Her voice was tinged with disgust. "That mouth of yours will get you fired, Strunk."

He pushed past them into the lobby.

Arledge motioned with her chin. "This way."

Together, they walked toward the wide front gate. As far as Kate knew, it was one of six gates in the sixteen-foot-high chain-link barrier that surrounded the compound. Miles of razor wire topped the fence all the way around the complex.

She shivered, partly from the cool air and partly from knowing the metal fence was wired with an electric current powerful enough to kill a person with one zap. She hugged her bag against her ribs. The spring morning was warm but not warm enough for the way she was dressed.

"This should be one of the best days of your life," Arledge said. "Forget Strunk. He's a jerk destined for self-destruction." She flipped a backhanded wave at the building.

"But you?" She looked at Kate. "You followed the rules, you completed the twelve-step recovery program, you attended chapel services and you were in the computer room almost every day doing classwork. Plus, you helped the other girls with their studies." She smiled. "I could tell you were trying to better yourself, and I wish you the best."

Kate studied the CO's eyes, seeing her in a new light. She'd had no idea the woman was observing her as well as guarding her. "I appreciate how you always treated us with respect," Kate said, "like we're human."

The officer tilted her head. "Can I ask you a question?"

"Sure."

"It's none of my business, but I'm curious to know where you're going from here."

Kate shrugged. Her plans were no secret. "I just completed a marketing degree online, but I still need to do a three-month internship, which will be at a Wyoming guest ranch called the Whispering Pines. I'll stay in Pittsburgh with my aunt for a few weeks and then drive west for the ranch's summer guest season."

Arledge's face brightened. "Congratulations, but..." Her brow furrowed. "Considering your circumstances, how was that approved?"

"Chaplain Sam says it was a God thing. The application form didn't have a section for arrest history and my advisor must not have mentioned my background. Or maybe she did, and the rancher hired me anyway."

"I bet it's pretty there."

Kate smiled. She couldn't help herself. "If it's anything like the pictures in their brochure, it's a beautiful ranch." She'd stared at the tiny pictures for hours, trying to imagine what it would be like to live in the mountains and wake up to such gorgeous scenery every morning.

They stopped at the brown guardhouse that sat just inside the fence. The red flowerbox beneath the austere building's window ledge looked to Kate like an afterthought meant to provide visitors with a positive first-impression of the prison. Purple and yellow pansies, their colorful faces lifted to the sun, were surrounded by a mix of white and lavender sweet alyssum. Some of the tiny blossoms draped over the side of the box.

Arledge turned to her. "The best of luck to you. Just remember, focus on your future, not your past."

"Thank you." Kate thought of Chaplain Sam's final words to her. *Live in the light, Kate. Bury the past and live in the light.*

The CO inside the guard house opened the window. "Good morning."

Arledge handed him Kate's ID tag. He made a notation on a chart before scanning the tag's information into a computer and depositing it in a drawer.

Kate assumed the scanner read her number as well as the awful picture that reflected how frightened and forlorn she'd felt the day it was taken. But that was old news. This was a new day and a new life.

Praying no last-minute glitches would prevent her release, she lowered the sack and held it with both hands. The bag was heavy. In addition to her toiletries, it contained her Bible plus several inspirational books Aunt Mary had sent through prison channels.

A breeze fluttered the flowers and goose-bumped Kate's arms. She breathed in the fragrant aroma. Pansies' happy faces always made her smile and she loved the smell of alyssum. But these flowers seemed out of place in the prison. In fact, they were the first flowers she'd seen at Patterson. The administration probably thought the inmates would smoke the leaves or stick them up their noses if they were accessible in the exercise yard.

Even so, she'd had flowers in her life. Kate smiled. Along with other minimum-security inmates, she had escaped Patterson's confines twice a week during the growing season to work at a community garden in the heart of Pittsburgh. Running soil through her fingers, planting seeds and pulling weeds calmed her spirit and reminded her that life went on outside prison walls.

The experience wasn't all sunshine and roses. Her orange-suited crew was routinely ridiculed by passersby, who called them names and spit at them. Some people even threw rocks. The abuse traumatized several of the inmates, who requested different work assignments.

But Kate had endured the same and worse when she worked the streets. For her, the few hours of normalcy, along with the joy of tending plants and working alongside volunteers who appreciated their help made it worth chancing an assault, verbal or otherwise.

The guard turned from the computer. "You're good to go." A buzzer sounded, and the pedestrian gate adjacent to the driveway gate slowly swung open.

"This is where Patterson State Penitentiary releases you back to the world," Arledge said. "Like I said, move forward with your life, not backward."

Kate responded with a solemn nod. "I will remember your words."

The officer pivoted and Kate hurried through the open gate. Another buzz, and it closed quietly behind her, unlike the noisy gates inside the facility. She glanced at the guard tower above her head. Although she couldn't see into the darkened windows, she knew at least one CO scrutinized her every move. Soon, she'd no longer be under twenty-four-seven surveillance.

A small car entered the large, crowded parking lot and slowly drove her direction. Was it Aunt Mary and Gertie Mae? Kate clasped her bag of books and toiletries close again. What was this jitter in her stomach? Excitement to finally be released? Anticipation to see her sweet aunt again? Or, was it fear of the future? She'd blown it so many times. Would she continue to mess up?

She thought again of Chaplain Sam, whose steady, wise counsel she would miss. "Once you belong to Christ," he'd said more than once in chapel, "it's not about what you can or can't do. It's what he can do in you and through you."

Sucking in a lungful of fresh air, she raised her face to the sun. Like the flowers that depended on God for sunshine and rain, she needed him now more than ever. Without him, she would wither into the addicted, delinquent person she was when she entered Patterson five years ago. "You know how weak I am, God," she whispered, "and how many times I've stumbled and fallen. Only you can keep me on my feet and on the right path."

A car horn honked.

Kate blinked and glanced around.

"Katy girl, over here, over here!"

She pivoted.

Her great-aunt was standing between cars in the middle of the lot, waving an arm high above her head.

No longer caring what the guards might think, Kate ran toward her aunt, her possessions tight against her chest. When she reached the car, she dropped the bag and hugged her aunt for the first time in years. Although Aunt Mary had been a frequent visitor, prison rules prohibited physical contact between inmates and visitors.

Kate held her fragile, precious aunt close. "I'm so happy to see you again, Aunt Mary." As always, her elderly relative, her only relative, smelled of wintergreen breath mints. She had "freshened her breath" with the pink Canada kind as long as Kate could remember.

"Katy, my sweet Katy!" Aunt Mary's sea-green eyes sparkled in the sunshine. She kissed Kate's cheek. "I'm so happy I can take you home today, sweetie. I hated all those times I visited and had to leave you behind. But Jesus answered my prayers, and today you're free for good."

"That's right." Kate reached for her bag. "I did my full time. No more Patterson, no parole, no parole officers." Only one caveat hung over her head. She was a two-time serious offender. Thanks to the "three strikes, you're out" law, one more arrest could mean she'd spend the remainder of her life behind bars.

But that wasn't going to happen, and it certainly wasn't something to think about right now. She opened the back door to put her things inside. Leaning in, she greeted Gertie Mae. "Thank you for coming to pick me up, Gertie. I really appreciate it."

"My pleasure." Gertie grinned. "I'd say, 'anytime,' but I'd rather not come here again, if you know what I mean."

Kate nodded and stepped around the door to help her aunt sit in the front seat and find her seatbelt. "I'm impressed you stood without your walker, Aunt Mary." Her aunt had had multiple sclerosis for years and was becoming more and more dependent on her walker and sometimes a wheelchair.

"I was too anxious to see you to bother with the walker. Besides, I had the door to hang onto." She looked Kate up and down.

Before her aunt could comment on the way she was dressed, Kate said, "I was super excited to see you, too." She closed the door and climbed into the backseat, pushing her bag and the folded walker to the other side. "Any chance we can stop by the DMV, Gertie? I need to pick up a driver's manual to study, so I can renew my driver's license."

Gertie backed out of the parking slot. "Sure, be glad to."

"First…" Mary touched Gertie's shoulder. "Let's stop by a department store to get Kate some warmer clothing."

"I have clothes at your house, Aunt Mary. I'll change when we—"

"The shopping trip is my treat, Katy dear." Mary peered around the headrest, waggling her finger. "I felt those goose bumps on your arms. We need to celebrate this wonderful occasion with a nice outfit you can wear to brunch. Gertie and I already picked the place. Right, Gert?"

Gertie glanced at Kate in the mirror. "You'll love it. They make the best omelets in town."

"No matter what they cook," Kate said, "I guarantee it'll be better than prison food." She twisted for one last glimpse of the penitentiary, surprised by the mix of emotions that flooded her chest.

Leaving the institution that had been her home for the past five years was a more nostalgic experience than she could have ever imagined. Not only was she leaving three squares and a cot behind, she'd left a circle of friends and a rigid routine. The security of knowing what tomorrow held—and the next day and the next—was something she hadn't had when she lived on the streets.

The car bumped out of the parking lot and onto the highway. She turned to face the front window. She would have Aunt Mary's prayers and support, like always, but the fact was, she was on her own again. Could she handle life on the outside? Or was Strunk right?

&

Kate swiveled one way, then the other, studying her reflection in the dressing room mirror. "What do you think, Amy?" She'd met Amy Iverson in prison. In no time, the two of them had become best friends who vowed to continue their friendship on the outside.

Amy grinned and tossed her auburn hair. "I love that shirt, Kate, and those Levis fit perfect." She pretended to aim a camera at Kate. "I can picture you sitting on a beautiful horse, dressed in those clothes plus the hat and boots the clerk took up front for you. Of course..." She winked. "A handsome cowboy would be seated next to you on a magnificent stallion. He'd notice how pretty you are and only have eyes for you."

Kate shook her head. Amy, the hopeless romantic, was fully aware she had no interest in men. "You need a new camera." She changed the subject. "I can't believe you found a western store in the middle of Pittsburgh. I love the leather smell here."

"Actually, I didn't find it. A guy I dated..." She made quotes with her fingers. "BP...was into western stuff."

Kate knew what she meant. "BP" was a common abbreviation among the inmates for "Before Patterson."

"He was into John Wayne and Clint Eastwood movies." Amy laughed. "We watched every single one of them, I think. Anyway, I came here a time or two with him, and I was always surprised at how busy the store was, like today."

"Who knew that locals have western yearnings?"

"Just like you." Amy grinned.

"Yeah, just like me. Three shirts should be plenty, don't you think? In addition to my other clothes, that is. Thank God I can finally fit into them again."

"You certainly worked hard enough to get back into shape. I lost ten pounds within the first two weeks after I got out, probably because I didn't eat all the carbs they fed us in prison. What's it been, a month since you were released?"

"Five weeks."

"You look great. And if you need more shirts, I'm sure you can buy what you need in Wyoming."

"After a paycheck or two." Kate turned for a last glance at herself, and her stomach did another flip-flop. Today, she could pass for the real deal, and soon she would be the real deal. She might not be an authentic cowgirl, but she'd be living and working on a Wyoming guest ranch.

Whispering Pines, here I come!

At lunch, Amy said, "This has been so much fun, Kate—not just being together again without COs hanging over us, acting like we're plotting to burn down the prison…"

A woman at the next table glanced at them then quickly turned her head.

Amy rolled her eyes. "I've never shopped with you before." She leaned closer and lowered her voice. "I mean, real shopping, not the commissary. That doesn't count. And we got to ride together on a bus that wasn't a work-crew bus."

"Yeah, it's been great," Kate said. "I appreciate all your help with decisions, 'cause I'm feeling a bit overwhelmed right now."

"I remember that feeling. When I got out, I wasn't sure which way to turn. Thank God I got the job at the horse stable, so I have some structure in my life. Plus, I can afford my own place and I don't have to live with my dad, which would have been miserable, at best. He'd nitpick my every breath and kick my dogs around." Her forehead puckered. "I hate to think what he'd do to my birds and cat."

"You've accumulated quite a menagerie in the short time you've been out."

"I already had my cat and the dogs. A friend kept them for me while I was in the pen. I got the birds to celebrate my release."

Kate reached for a cucumber slice topped with cream cheese, a sprinkle of herbs and a carrot curl. "We can thank Aunt Mary for the shopping spree and for lunch. She even made the reservations for this place."

"I wondered why you picked it, 'cause it's a bit girlie…" Amy deepened her voice. "For a couple tough-as-nails ex-cons like us."

The woman next to them shifted her chair farther away from their table.

Amy snickered. "But it's nice. You'd think we were inside a quaint little English cottage. And it smells delicious in here, like crumpets and strawberry jam, or whatever they eat over in the mother country." She pooched her bottom lip. "I just wish your aunt had come with us. She's such a darling."

"She wanted us to have a 'besties day out,' as she called it." Kate wiped the smear of cream cheese she could feel at the corner of her lips. "I think she learned that word from the girls in the fifth-grade Sunday school class she teaches. But mostly, it was the multiple sclerosis that kept her home. She tires easily and was worried about getting on and off a bus with her walker. I offered to bring her wheelchair, but she didn't want to bother with it."

"What do you think of this idea?" Amy leaned across the table. "Like I told you, I'm planning to buy my cousin's car when I have enough saved for a down payment, which should be soon. He said I can pay the rest month by month. What if I drove your aunt to Wyoming to visit you? After you get settled, of course." She gave Kate a side glance. "You know I'm dying to see the ranch—and all those good-looking cowboys."

"Aunt Mary would love that, and so would I." Kate grinned. "I'm sure the cowboys would be thrilled to meet you, too."

Amy lifted a flowered teacup from a gold-edged saucer and crooked her little finger. "Here's to the two of us living the good life on the outside, and to your grand Wyoming adventure."

Raising her cup, Kate said, "Oh, give me a home, where the buffalo roam—and where my best friend comes to visit me soon."

❧

Kate closed her Honda's hood, wiped her fingers on a paper towel and got inside the car to test the new battery. Pleased the motor turned over on the first try, she backed out of the garage onto the driveway, set the brake and turned off the engine. With the new license plate and a screwdriver in hand, she knelt behind the car to remove the outdated plate.

The next-door neighbor boy, Jake, stopped bouncing a basketball against his parents' house and wandered over. "Want me to help you?" Sunshine brightened his copper hair.

"Sure." Kate handed him the screwdriver. "You can loosen the screws for me."

After they'd removed the old plate and Kate was pulling the new one from the envelope, Jake asked, "Are you going to live with Miss Mary now?"

"Only for a short time. I'll be working on a Wyoming guest ranch over the summer."

Jake's eyes widened above his freckled cheeks. "With real cowboys?"

"It's a working guest ranch that has horses and cattle and even bison, so I suspect they'll have a cowboy or two to keep track of the animals."

"Cool."

"Aunt Mary told me you mow and water her lawn in the summer, rake her leaves in the fall and shovel her walks in the winter. I really appreciate you doing that for her."

"I don't mind." He ducked his head. "She gives me lemonade and hot chocolate and cookies—and pays me five dollars. But I'd do it even if she didn't pay me, 'cause she's so nice."

"She's a special lady, and I know your family will watch over her when I'm gone, like you always have." Guilt plucked Kate's heartstrings. She was her aunt's only living relative. She should be the one taking care of her. In fact, she'd offered to find a local business for the internship, but Aunt Mary was as excited as she was for her to go to Wyoming. Kate had a feeling she wanted her to get as far away from her old crowd as possible.

She rubbed at a rust spot on the trunk. Thanks to being locked inside the garage for the past few years, the car didn't have much more rust than it had before she was arrested. However, she'd had to dig a mouse nest out of the backseat and vacuum hundreds of droppings.

Amy said they used aluminum foil at the stable to discourage mice from making new nests. And Aunt Mary had told her mice hate the smell of peppermint. Taking their advice, Kate stuffed the hole in the upholstery with a big wad of foil plus a cotton ball saturated with peppermint oil and spread a blanket across the seat. If nothing else, the car smelled better.

"Were you living in Wyoming before?" Jake gave her a shy glance. "I haven't seen you in a long time."

"No. I'm sorry to say I've been in prison, a place I trust you'll never go."

"That's what I thought," Jake said, "'cause I heard my mom talking to your aunt once and she said something about prison. So, that's what I told the man."

20

Kate frowned. "What man?"

"A guy in a uniform. He came here two times." Jake held up two fingers. "Well, I talked to him two times. He could have come more."

"Was he a policeman?"

"No, the writing on the sleeve said he was from a prison, but I don't remember which one."

"What color was his uniform?"

"The pants were dark and the shirt was a lighter color, kind of like this shirt I'm wearing." He poked his forefinger into the middle of his gray t-shirt.

Patterson COs wore gray, but Kate had never heard of them doing house calls. "Did he wear a big black belt with pouches on it?"

"Yeah, and he kept patting his gun, almost like he was trying to scare me."

Kate tilted her head. Patterson guards didn't carry weapons. "Can you describe his face?"

Jake squinted at her like she was giving him the third degree, which she was. "Sorry," Kate said. "I'm just trying to figure out why someone from the prison I was in would be asking you about me while I was still there. Doesn't make sense."

"I guess not." Jake scratched his head. "His hair was black and shiny-like. And combed the same as the Fonzie guy on that old TV show my mom watches. He wasn't real tall, but taller than you, I think."

Kate sucked in a breath. She knew a former CO who fit that description.

Jake raised his eyebrows. "Do you know him?"

"Maybe." She shrugged. "Anything else?"

"Well…" The boy thought for a moment. "Oh, yeah. He smelled. Whew, did he smell!"

"Like he hadn't showered?"

"No, like he used too much of that stuff men put on after they shave. My dad only uses a little and my mom says she likes it. But this guy…" Jake pinched his nose.

Kate picked up the screwdriver. The guard she was thinking of drenched himself in Brut. But he'd been fired months ago by the prison and would no longer have a uniform. Unless…unless he'd somehow managed to keep one for whatever nefarious con-job he might concoct in the future. She stood. What in the world did he want with her?

Jake got to his feet. "Did Miss Mary tell you he knocked on her door and talked to her?"

"He did?" Kate stared at the boy. "What did he say to her?"

"All I heard was that he wanted to make sure her niece didn't return to her old ways, whatever that means."

"Did you hear my aunt's reply?"

"Her voice was too soft, but I think she said something about Wyoming."

If the man was who she thought he was, Kate didn't like him being anywhere near her aunt—or Jake. She hated that her past behavior put others in potential danger. "Did you see what kind of car he drove?"

"It was a brown pickup truck. Not real old, but not new, either."

"Did it have the prison name on the side?"

"No…" Jake's brow furrowed. "That's weird, huh?"

"Yeah, that is strange. Do you remember anything else about the man?"

"He didn't seem like a nice person." Jake bounced his ball on the cement. "He sort of scared me."

Kate nodded. "I understand." During her years of living on the streets plus jail and prison stints, she'd met plenty of people whose demeanor frightened her. They didn't have to say a word. She just knew to avoid them, which wasn't always possible, especially with men like the one Jake described.

"He asked if you had a car. I said 'yes,' and he wanted to know where you keep it. I told him it was in there." Jake pointed at the garage. "I see it when I get the snow shovel and the rake. Miss Mary told me it was yours. After I showed him, he walked around the garage, like three times, and even peeked in the window."

Bouncing the ball again, he said, "And he had on black boots."

Kate bent down to make sure the last screw was tight. "Thanks for your help, Jake, and for telling me about that guy. Please let me know if you see him again."

"Yeah, sure."

"I believe Aunt Mary has some peanut butter cookies in her cookie jar." Kate smiled. "Can I interest you in a couple?"

After she and Aunt Mary washed the supper dishes that evening, Kate filled the teapot, set it on the stove and turned the knob to high. She pulled two mugs from the cupboard before she sat across from her aunt at the kitchen table. "Jake helped me put the license plate on my car this afternoon. He's a sweet kid."

"Yes, he's a wonderful boy," Aunt Mary said. "He's been a big help to me." She straightened the paper napkins in the holder that had sat in the middle of the table for as long as Kate could remember. "Did I tell you that Gertie drove your car around the neighborhood once a month before the license expired? She thought that would keep it in good running condition."

"No, you didn't tell me." Kate smiled. "That was really thoughtful. I'll have to thank her." She pulled chamomile tea bags from a box and placed them in the cups. "Jake told me a man in a uniform was here asking about me. He talked with Jake and also knocked on your door. Do you remember that?"

"Yes, I do." Mary nodded. "It was shortly before you were released. His uniform was similar to those the guards at your prison wear."

Ignoring the urge to tell her aunt that Patterson was no longer "her" prison, she asked, "What did he want?"

"I'm not sure." Mary rubbed her chin. "He seemed confused about when you were getting out, so I told him."

"That's all he wanted to know?"

"He was quite curious about your plans for the future. But even though he was a prison official, I didn't like the looks of him—or his smell. He must have bathed in cologne." She wrinkled her nose. "I told him you were going to Wyoming, so he wouldn't come here thinking he could find you after you were released.

"But…" Her eyebrows tightened. "Maybe I didn't do the right thing. Maybe I told him too much. I wanted to be honest so you wouldn't get in trouble with the law again."

Kate got up to hug her aunt. "What you said was perfect." If the man was who she thought he was, knowing she'd moved away would keep him from bothering Aunt Mary. "Please let me know if he returns."

The tea kettle began to vibrate. Kate turned it off before the whistle reached siren level. Her aunt said the loud noise was helpful when she was in another room, but the intensity could be ear-splitting. She poured the boiling water over chamomile tea bags and checked her watch so she wouldn't steep the tea too long. Aunt Mary, who was as mild-mannered and easy-going as a kitten, had specific requirements when it came to tea.

Kate stirred honey into each cup. In a moment, she'd add the dab of cream her aunt liked in her tea. She inhaled the soothing aroma, wishing she could tell Aunt Mary to call the police if the ex-CO knocked on her door again. But that would alarm her, and she would ask questions, questions Kate preferred not to answer.

Winds of Hope

❧

Leaving her dear, sweet aunt and her best friend behind was hard for Kate. Amy had arrived at six a.m. for breakfast and they'd all shed tears when Kate said her final goodbyes two hours later. But she'd see them soon. And she'd call them daily to give them a trip update.

Kate didn't relax until she'd crossed the Pennsylvania/West Virginia border on I-70 and had driven the fifteen or so miles into Ohio. She wasn't far from home, yet being two states away somehow helped her psyche accept the fact she was no longer a ward of the State of Pennsylvania. Ditching her past and the man who'd been asking about her allowed her to breathe a bit easier.

Her little red Honda wasn't the speediest car on the road, yet the wind in her hair, her favorite music on the radio, and knowing she could go anywhere and do anything she wanted made the miles fly by. She'd never been outside Pittsburgh city limits. Every mile of scenery along I-70 was new to her. She reveled in the spring green that colored the fields and tinged the hills and the trees. She gloried in the fresh smell of new life that blew in the window—and the daffodils and tulips that graced the rest stops.

Her only regret was that I-70 would take her through large cities—Columbus, Indianapolis, Kansas City and Denver. She'd spent her entire life in a big city. Time for a change.

But that would come soon enough. She'd leave the interstate somewhere west of Denver and drive two-lane highways to her final destination. Although the ranch was in Wyoming, it was situated near the Colorado border, not far from Steamboat Springs.

Aunt Mary had packed enough food for three people and given her cash for gas and lodging. If she could have made it to Wyoming without her aunt's money, Kate would have refused it. However, licensing and insuring her car plus paying for new tires and minor repairs had added up. The expenditures consumed her commissary check as well as most of the funds in the account where the state had deposited her work-crew income. She'd been paid less than fifty cents an hour, which wasn't a lot, but it was better than nothing.

When her aunt gave her the money, she said, "This makes up for not being allowed to raise you when you were young. The state thought my age and health would hinder me. I know I could have taken care of you, with God's help, but apparently, that wasn't meant to be." She smiled and patted Kate's cheek. "Consider this your college fund, sweetie."

Her aunt's unspoken intention, Kate knew, was to prevent her from running low on funds and reverting to the thievery and other illicit activities that had landed her behind bars time and time again.

ℒ

Not far from St. Louis, Kate stopped at a motel in Illinois where she had a reservation. She got out of the car and stretched her back, studying the tall building. After all the negative encounters she'd had in motels during her BP days, she had considered driving straight through or sleeping in her car. But Aunt Mary insisted she stay in a motel, a nice one. This one would meet her approval.

Ignoring the tremor in her stomach, she grabbed her purse and suitcase and rolled it into a lobby crowded with people and luggage. The purse strap riding on her shoulder felt odd. Even if purses had been allowed in prison, she'd had no use for one there.

She stopped at the rear of the long line and waited, grateful she had a reservation and more than ready for a relaxing hot shower. When she reached the counter, the clerk, an older man with beautiful white hair, perfect teeth and a carnation in his lapel, greeted her with a smile. But after a quick check of his computer, he informed her she'd lost the reservation. She hadn't called to say she would arrive after six.

"I don't travel much," Kate said. Understatement of the century. "If I'd known, I would have checked in before I gassed my car and ate."

The man offered a sympathetic smile. "I'm sorry about the confusion. Tell you what, miss. I'll give you a voucher for a free stay the next time you come through here. A return trip, perhaps?"

"I need a place to stay tonight. I can sleep in my car if I have to, but I'd rather not." Her dream of a hot shower was quickly sliding down the drain.

He turned his attention to the computer screen again.

Kate hoped he'd see he was mistaken, but he shook his head.

"I'm afraid," he said, "that all of the three-, four- and five-star accommodations in the area are booked." He glanced at her over his bifocals. "That's due to our annual tulip festival, which happens to be this week. People come from all over. It's quite a celebration."

Despite the growing line behind her, Kate put her hands on the counter. "I'm willing to stay at a one- or two-star place. All I need is a bed. Nothing fancy. Can you check your computer for me, please?"

He started clicking again, his eyes shifting back and forth as he read the screen. He frowned.

"What?"

"There's one room left in town, but I wouldn't recommend a nice young lady like you take it. The facility is on the seamy side of the city."

Seamy side of town? She'd done plenty of seamy. And she wasn't the nice girl he thought she was. "Would you please call and tell them I'll be there as fast as I can drive there?"

He peered at her beneath his thick white eyebrows. "Are you sure, miss? As I said, it's an unsavory sort of place."

"I know martial arts." She bent closer. "I can take care of myself."

A doubtful expression flicked across his face. "Why don't I call my wife and ask if—"

Kate shook her head. "Thank you for your concern, but I'd appreciate directions to the hotel. What's the name?"

"Drag-In Bar and Hotel."

"Drag-In?"

"I believe it's a play on words. Their logo has a dragon on it. It's not a pleasant locale. You'd be better off driving to the next—"

"Where is it?"

He sighed and told her how to get there, then lifted the phone again. She thanked him, grabbed her suitcase handle and hurried past curious stares. The automatic doors swished open before her.

The Drag-In Bar and Hotel's faded front door was propped open by a barstool with a torn cushion. Light from the setting sun highlighted smeared fingerprints around the edges of the door. Kate jerked her suitcase over the half-rotted threshold and squinted, adjusting to the dim lighting beyond the swath of sunshine.

One of her street friends had once said, "If it doesn't smell like puke and piss, it ain't a dive bar." This one definitely qualified for "dive." She hated to admit it, but the stinky, smoky place felt like home, a home she hadn't visited for several years. After the long drive, the thought of sitting down with a cold beer—

"You the one who wants the room?"

She turned in the direction of the voice. A hazy but bulky male figure was outlined by the soft glow coming from the mirror behind the bar. "Yes. My name is Kate, Kate Neilson." In the corner, a jukebox flashed muted rainbow colors and someone—she couldn't tell if the person was male or female—slouched in a nearby booth.

"Want to see it first?"

"Does it have clean sheets?"

"Far as I know."

"I'll take it."

The room didn't cost much, which made Kate feel like she was handling Aunt Mary's money wisely. But the low price made her nervous. How bad was the room?

Trailing behind the man, Kate bumped her suitcase up two flights of stairs. When they reached the second landing, he turned down a long hallway that was almost as smoky as the bar. The suitcase wheels rattled over the uneven floor.

At the end of the hall, the bartender stopped before a dingy door and inserted a key. At first it didn't work, but he jiggled the key several times and the lock released. He didn't wait for her to enter. Instead, he stepped inside to switch on a lamp and open the drapes. Late-afternoon sunlight accented the nose prints on the dirty window.

"Phone's over there by the bed." He pointed at the nightstand. "If you need anything, dial zero and I'll answer...until two a.m., that is. After that, you're on your own." He plopped a bottle of water on the nightstand and handed her the key. "Water's on the house. It's cold. If you need more, call me."

As soon as the big man left, Kate triple-locked the door and hurried to the window. The place reeked of cigarettes and body odor. She flipped the latch then slid the window as far as she could, which wasn't far. But at least it allowed a breeze to flow into the stuffy room. She twisted her torso to lean her head and shoulder out.

Below her, a fire escape ran beneath the window, and below that, a mangy dog sniffed the trash bins that studded the alley. A huge, rusted, metal building sat across the alley. Above it hung a darkening but clear blue sky.

Kate straightened. Not bad for the unsavory, seamy side of town. She'd seen worse, much worse. She turned from the window to survey the room. Not bad at all. It even had a beach picture hanging over the bed, but...

She glanced from one side of the small, musty room to the other. Where was the bathroom? In the hall? After she unhooked the chain lock, released the deadbolt and unlocked the doorknob, she peeked into the hallway but saw no sign of a bathroom.

Frowning, she redid the locks and picked up the corded phone. The bartender answered on the third ring. "Yeah?"

"Where's the restroom?"

"At the end of the hall."

"I didn't see it."

"The other end."

Someone must have put money in the jukebox, because she heard a drumroll through the phone, followed by a guitar twang. "Do you have any rooms with bathrooms?"

He grunted. "You got the best room in the house, sister."

Kate replaced the phone in the receiver. So, that's why the room was so cheap. She sighed and reminded herself she'd told the first clerk all she needed for the night was a bed—and that he'd said this was the only room left in town.

Pulling back the covers, she sniffed the threadbare sheet, made a face and stood. She would cover the pillow with a towel, if the bathroom had clean ones, or her jacket while she slept.

She unfolded the luggage rack and set her suitcase on it without opening it. The less exposure to smoky air the better. Her original plan had been to check into the hotel and then return to the car to get the muffins and fruit her aunt had packed for her breakfast.

But she knew better than to walk through the bar again. The temptation to have "just one beer" was too strong. Stopping at one had never been her strong point. She'd eat breakfast in the car while she drove tomorrow.

Because the room had no chair, she sat on the end of the bed and dialed her aunt's number on the cell phone she'd purchased shortly before the trip. Aunt Mary answered almost immediately. "Is this my sweet Katy?"

Kate smiled. Her aunt had been sitting by the phone, waiting for her call. "It's me, Aunt Mary. I stopped in western Illinois for the night, just before the Missouri border."

"Sounds like you're making excellent progress. Did you have a good trip?"

"Yes. Spring is everywhere. I've seen calves and lambs and baby goats playing in the fields alongside the highway, and I've also seen lots of flowers, including daffodils and tulips. In fact, this town is hosting a tulip festival right now. I might check it out before I leave tomorrow."

"That's wonderful. Is your motel room nice?"

The edge of the drape ruffled with the breeze.

"It's not fancy, but it's adequate." Kate stood and walked over to the window. "I'm ready for a good night's sleep." A bass thump from the music downstairs rattled the window. She'd been able to sleep through a blaring television and bickering women while in prison. She could sleep through this.

"I'll let you go then. This is your nickel."

Kate grinned. Her aunt was still counting pennies for her—or in this case, nickels. But she couldn't let her off the line quite yet. "Has that prison guard knocked on your door again, Aunt Mary?"

"No, I haven't seen him. Why do you ask?"

"I just want to be sure he's not bothering you, that's all."

"I told him you were leaving. He has no reason to come around here."

Kate prayed that was the case, but she hadn't forgotten how persistent he could be.

"I'd better let you go. Sleep tight, sweetie."

"You, too, Aunt Mary. I love you."

"I love you, too, and I'll be anticipating a call from you tomorrow evening."

After they said their goodbyes, Kate called Amy, who didn't answer, so she left a message. Amy had told her she'd be working late due to a horse show and might not be able to answer her phone.

Kate laid her phone on the bedside stand and checked her watch, which now worked, thanks to a new battery. She was tired, but it wasn't dark yet. After a trip to the bathroom to brush her teeth and wash her face, she would read a few chapters in the Billy Graham book Gertie had given her as a going-away gift. Tomorrow night, when she had a private bathroom, would be a better time for a shower.

She gathered her things, including her purse and the sheathed knife she'd dug out of a box in the back of her car before entering the bar. She'd found it in Aunt Mary's attic and recognized it as her Great-Uncle Dean's hunting knife. Slipping it into her purse, she switched off the lamp and stepped into the hallway. She pulled the locked door shut behind her and started toward the bathroom.

Televisions announced their presence in some of the rooms along the way and snores and conversations came from others, but no one was in the hall. The closer she got to her destination, the louder the music grew. Maybe she did have the best room in the place—the one farthest from the bar noise.

The bathroom door was open. Kate stuck her head in, fearful of what she might find. Like her room, the bathroom wasn't fancy, but it appeared clean. She stepped inside and locked the door. The white washcloths and towels, though almost as thin as prison towels, were stain-free and smelled okay, if she ignored the hint of smoke. And the combination bathtub/shower was spotless. Sampler-size soap bars and small bottles of conditioning shampoo sat on the counter next to the sink.

Why not? She kicked off her sandals and slipped her t-shirt over her head. Nothing like a shower to relax after a long day in the car.

By the time Kate towel-dried her long hair and dressed, the light coming through the opaque window was fading into dusk. As she was about to leave, she pulled a dry towel from the rack to cover the pillow in her room, hung it on her arm and exited the restroom, purse and toiletry bag in hand.

This time, she heard voices downstairs and the music was louder. But again, the hallway was empty. She had a feeling that as the evening progressed, the place would come alive. In her tired state, she'd probably sleep through the commotion.

Unlocking her room required a great deal of key wiggling, like before. She was glad she'd watched the bartender work the lock. Finally, she was able to twist the knob and push the door open. She stepped inside, closed the door and was reaching for the chain lock when a hand covered her mouth and an arm clamped across her chest.

Kate dropped her things and drove her elbow into the intruder's ribs.

He gasped, wheezing alcohol breath, and loosened his hold.

Spinning around, Kate thrust her other elbow upward into his chin.

The man staggered backward, landing with his back on the bed.

She kicked him in the groin for good measure.

He moaned, reached for his crotch and crumpled to the floor.

Kate switched on the lamp, whipped the knife from her purse on the floor and unsheathed it. Standing above the motionless man, breathing hard, she examined him in the lamplight. Skinny and pock-faced, he had a sharp nose and greasy blond hair that fell over his eyes. She'd never seen him before.

She stared from the window to the door. How did he get in her room? The door was locked, but he could have easily jimmied the flimsy lock, snuck inside and relocked it. A wind gust fluttered the drape. She should have closed the window…yet, she was on the third floor. Even with a fire escape, how did a drunk man climb that high and squeeze through the narrow opening?

She stared at the window and then at the man. Was she a random target or did he know what room she was in—and that she was gone, taking a shower? The only one who knew her room number or that she'd asked about the bathroom was the bartender. Oh, yeah…and the person she'd noticed in the booth by the jukebox.

Stepping over his inert body, she reached for the phone on the nightstand but then hesitated, hand in midair. Had the bartender sent him to her room to steal her valuables? She shook her head. As big as the bartender was, he didn't need for someone else to do his dirty work. Of course, that would keep his hands clean if the person was caught.

She dropped her hand. What now? Calling the police was out of the question. An ex-con/former prostitute who'd just been released from prison would either be ignored by the authorities or arrested for solicitation and assault. With

38

her "three strikes, you're out" status, she couldn't take any chances.

Kneeling beside the man, who showed no sign of awareness, she watched his chest rise and fall twice. Thank God he was alive, even though he smelled half-dead. She stepped over him again and walked to the window to suck in a breath of air. A homicide charge would not be good. Not good at all. She stuck her head through the opening and peered along the fire-escape walkway. A drape blew out of a window at the far end.

She straightened. Maybe he was sitting on the fire escape and saw her open window. But he was inebriated and couldn't have known she'd only be gone a short while. Maybe he happened to look out his door when she was walking to the bathroom.

He moaned and Kate turned. Where the creep came from didn't matter. She wanted him out of her room. Now. She laid the knife on the window ledge and crawled across the bed to snatch the bottled water from the nightstand. It was no longer ice-cold, but that was okay. It was cold enough. She twisted the cap off the bottle.

The man shifted.

Kate retrieved the knife and moved to stand above the intruder. Holding the bottle over him, she tilted it.

The water splashed onto his face, and his eyes blinked open.

She brandished the knife. "Get out."

He squinted at her, mouth open.

She dumped the rest of the water on him.

He sputtered and tried to sit up but then yelped and grasped his crotch.

Kate towered over the scrawny, squirming man, the water bottle in one hand and the hunting knife in the other. "I can finish what I started…" She thrust the knife at him.

He scooted back, his gaze shifting between the knife, her face and the door.

"Or I can call that big burly bartender downstairs to deal with you however he pleases…"

His eyes widened. "No," he stammered. "I'll leave." He tried to get up but groaned and fell back against the bed.

"Or, better yet, I'll call the cops. I have a feeling they know you well."

"No! I have money."

She threw the bottle at him.

He flinched.

"I don't want your drug money. But I bet the cops would like to get their hands on it—and you." She reached for the phone.

He rolled over, and on hands and knees started for the door.

"Stop."

He kept going.

Kate kicked him, knocking him into the clothes strewn about the room. For the first time, she noticed he'd emptied her suitcase.

He lay on his side, shaking.

"You know what I want?" She waved the hunting knife.

He didn't respond, just eyed the knife.

"I want you out of here as much as you want out of here. Tell you what..." She picked up the phone, waited several moments, and then dropped it back into the receiver. "You leave the way you came, and we'll both be happy."

His wide-ranging expressions almost made her laugh. Hope. Disbelief. Relief. Suspicion.

He glanced at the window before pointing a trembling finger at the door.

Kate shook her head and indicated the window with the knife. "Get. Out. Now. Before I change my mind." She inched closer to the phone.

He twisted to his knees and crawled toward the window, moaning with every movement. Kate didn't know much about anatomy, but she had a feeling swelling had set in.

Grasping the window ledge, the intruder pulled himself up. Again, he stared longingly at the door.

Kate stepped from beside the bed and stood between him and the door. She motioned with the knife. "Go."

His already pallid features paled. He shoved the window to open it farther, but it barely budged.

Good, thought Kate, more fingerprints. Just in case she needed proof of breaking and entering.

He turned sideways, put one leg over the ledge, let out a garbled scream and fell onto the fire escape, one foot still inside.

Shoving his foot out, she slammed the window shut, latched it and yanked the curtains closed. Despite the wall between them, she could hear him cursing her and calling her vile names. She turned her back—and the room closed in on her.

Kate frowned at the bed. She couldn't sleep here. This was a return to her old world, her old nightmares. For all she knew, the jerk would return with a weapon or an accomplice. She couldn't stay. Even if he didn't come back, she wouldn't be able to sleep.

Her heart pounded. Her hands shook. She needed a drink or a hit, something to calm her mind and body. Kate gathered her things from the floor and threw them in the suitcase. Purse, water bottle and room key in hand—and the knife's leather sheath between her spine and the back of her pants, she opened the door and checked the hallway.

Again, she saw no one. And she no longer heard her assailant's yells. Was he still on the fire escape? Or was he in a nearby room? Either way, he was likely curled in a fetal position.

Rather than banging her suitcase down the stairs one by one, she carried it. This was not the time to call attention to herself. The smoke grew denser and the music louder with each step. She realized no one could hear her, yet she continued to carry the suitcase. At the landing, she stopped to survey the packed bar. The jukebox pulsed and a disco ball, something she hadn't seen in years, rained sparkles on the handful of dancers swaying in place on the small dance floor.

From a nearby table, a man got up and staggered her direction. Before he could reach her, Kate wheeled her suitcase across the room. The bartender, who'd been talking with two men seated at the bar, turned to her. "Ah, Ms. Neilson. What can I get you?"

The other men eyed her, curious expressions on their faces.

Kate cringed. He'd remembered her name—and shared it with his audience of two. She held up the water bottle. "Would you please refill this for me?"

"I can do better than that." He opened a cooler, pulled out a fresh bottle and set it on the counter with a thump. "Can I get you anything else? This is two-for-one night. Buy a house beer and get one free."

Kate tilted her head. Two for one? A cold beer—two cold beers—would be heavenly right now. Just what she needed. She slid onto a stool. "Sounds good."

The bartender held a mug under the tap and pulled the handle. A spurt of liquid bubbled out, then nothing more. "End of that," he said. "I've filled a lot of mugs tonight. But no worries. We have refrigerated cans in the back. I'll go get you a couple." He pushed through swinging doors at the side of the bar.

What are you doing?

Kate turned to the two men, but they were deep in conversation and no one sat on the other side of her.

You promised.

And she knew. She'd heard that voice before, a voice that had come to her more than once after she met Jesus in prison. She sighed. *Yes, I promised. I'm sorry.*

The bartender returned and plopped two cans in front of her.

Kate swallowed. "Thanks, but I changed my mind. That's not why I'm here."

"What?" He squinted at her.

She held up the room key. "I'm checking out."

He arched a thick eyebrow. "Something wrong with the room?"

"Couldn't sleep." She shrugged. "But that's okay. I need to get down the road."

He studied her for a moment. "Did you use the shower?"

She nodded.

He opened the cash register drawer and pulled out the check-in form she'd signed, along with several bills. "Here's your money back, minus five dollars for the shower. Fair deal?"

"Fair deal." Kate laid the key on the counter and stuffed the cash in her pocket along with the check-in form.

"Sure you don't want the beer? As long as you don't open the cans, you can take them with you."

"Want? Yes. Need? No." Ignoring his mystified expression, she took the cold, damp water bottle, grabbed her suitcase and hurried out the door. As she maneuvered past a cluster of men wrapped in a smoke cloud, someone called, "Hey, baby, I'll buy you a drink."

Kate ran for her car. She hated that her hands were full, which wasn't safe, and that she had to fumble in her purse for keys. As fast as her quivering fingers allowed, she unlocked the car, heaved her suitcase into the Honda's hatchback and slammed it shut. Jumping into the front, she tossed her purse and the water bottle onto the passenger seat and locked the doors.

With a quick glance at the rearview mirror, she started the engine and backed from the slot. Gunning the motor, she flew out of the parking lot, tires squealing. She was tired but wide awake and so, so glad to escape her past, again. No more grungy hotels for her. And no more bars.

Ten minutes later, Kate spotted a fast-food restaurant with a brightly lit parking lot and stopped long enough to find the interstate on her phone's map. Before she took off, she reached behind her back to retrieve the sheathed knife, which was rubbing a sore spot on her spine. She laid it beside her purse.

Once she was on the highway, the uneasiness in her stomach subsided and she settled deeper into the well-worn seat with a sigh of relief. *Thank you, Lord, for getting me out of that place without any cop encounters—and for saving me from addiction, again.*

All she'd left behind was a name the bartender would soon forget, a few fingerprints and one miserable man. If he had any sense at all in his pickled brain, he'd never again assume women were weak, easy prey. Maybe, like her, he'd even decide to forsake his criminal behavior and become a law-abiding citizen.

Yet, the fact was, she was as hopelessly addicted as the jerk who'd accosted her. She rubbed her nose. She could still smell him. But she wasn't any better than he was. Despite all the recovery groups and addiction classes in prison, she'd almost succumbed to alcoholism again. Thanks to God's intervention, she hadn't drunk the beers.

On the outskirts of St. Louis, she spied a Best Western with a flashing vacancy sign just off the freeway. Too tired to drive any farther, she took the next exit ramp and pulled into the motel's parking lot. Inside, the desk clerk, a young woman, glanced at the clock on the wall. "Because it's so late, I can extend your checkout time. However, I can't give you the entire day."

"That's really nice of you," Kate said. "But I hope to be out of here no later than nine. Can you arrange for a wakeup call at nine, in case I oversleep?"

"I'll be glad to." She typed something into the computer. "The breakfast bar is open from five a.m. to nine. If it's closed when you come down, you can still grab a granola bar and coffee."

"Great. Thank you." Kate rolled her suitcase onto the elevator, rested her head against the wall and closed her eyes. When she heard a ding, she blinked and saw a red "5" illuminated above the door. She'd come close to falling asleep standing up.

The room smelled clean and welcoming. Kate locked the door and checked the window before she tucked the knife under a pillow and slipped between the bedcovers. She didn't awaken until she heard voices in the hallway. Groaning, she blinked at the clock. Ten 'til nine.

Tempted to sleep longer, she decided a quick shower sounded better. Not that many hours had passed since her last shower. In theory, she was clean, but the cigarette smoke that still clung to her hair made her feel dirty. If only she could wash the bar smells from her clothes.

On the way to her car, she grabbed the promised coffee and granola bar in the breakfast room and walked out into the sunshine, ready to face a new day and excited to be on her way again.

Winds of Hope

From St. Louis, Kate headed across Missouri into Kansas, her anticipation growing by the mile. She would pass the halfway mark soon, and not long after that, she'd see the Rocky Mountains for the first time. She couldn't wait. Yet, she sensed a dark undercurrent beneath her excitement. What could that mean?

Sipping juice and munching one of Aunt Mary's chocolate chip cookies as she drove, she came to a conclusion, one that surprised her. The butterflies in her stomach originated from nervousness as well as anticipation. She was walking into a man's world.

The woman she'd talked with from the ranch, Laura Duncan, seemed nice enough. But Kate knew she'd be working with seasoned ranch hands who might not appreciate a female joining the staff, if they were anything like male correctional officers. Although the bulk of her work would be in the office, Laura had said she could assist with trail rides now and then and might even be called on to help in other areas of the ranch. "I tell the staff we're all in it together," she'd said. "The goal is to have a successful guest season."

Kate liked Laura's philosophy. She'd already decided she wouldn't mind rubbing shoulders with the ranch hands and helping them with their work. In fact, she relished the idea. The Whispering Pines staff would soon learn she was no threat to their male-dominated culture. Between jail and prison, street life and foster homes, she'd had her fill of men. She wouldn't interfere with their lives or their work—

unless, of course, one of them accosted her. Like the man at the hotel, he'd learn a quick lesson.

Kate slapped her cheek and glanced in the mirror. What was with the negativity all of a sudden? She blew out a long sigh. The encounter at the Drag-In had unsettled her more than she realized.

Life on a Wyoming ranch would be far different from the life she'd experienced in Pittsburgh. She was sure of it. Foster families, drug dealers, gangs, pimps, johns and prison guards were all behind her, including the one who talked with Jake and Aunt Mary. A much better life awaited her, a happy life, one she'd dreamed of since childhood.

Kate grinned and honked the horn long and loud. "Whispering Pines, here I come!"

CYRUS

CYRUS MOORE STEPPED OUT OF his ranch house onto the front porch, a beer in one hand and a cigarette in the other. The screen door slammed behind him.

Slick, his border collie, was sleeping in the far corner. The dog raised his head and sniffed the air. Cyrus sometimes gave him pieces of whatever he was eating, so he knew that was what the dog was hoping for. But when no food scraps came his way, Slick dropped his chin to his paws and closed his eyes.

Cyrus blew out a puff of smoke and inhaled the evening air. No rain in the breeze tonight. He rested a shoulder against the support post and watched the top rim of the sun dip behind the canyon wall.

The striated red rocks stained with black streaks served as an ever-present yet ever-changing backdrop for the cottonwoods that followed the creek, the newly greened hayfield and his rustic barn. Now hidden, the sun cast spears of light into the clouds, varnishing his grandparents' homestead with a golden glow.

With a groan and a crunch from his bad knee, Cyrus settled into the lone rocking chair and set the bottle on the wooden crate beside it. He took a long drag of cigarette smoke, leaned his head against the chair back and blew smoke rings at the porch roof. The calm, warm evening was a long-time-in-comin' letup from the north wind that had blasted down the canyon all winter long.

But as much as he hankered for springtime during those endless frigid months, sitting on the porch, staring across the home place, always set his mind to wandering through the plains of his past. But maybe this spring and this summer would be different. He was getting up in years. It was time to leave the dadgum bygone days behind.

The fledgling leaves on the tall cottonwood that shaded the porch in the summer rattled with a wind gust. His grandfather had transplanted the tree from beside the creek the day after he and the neighbors finished building the house. It was ancient, as cottonwoods go, but still standing, a testimony to Cyrus's heritage. He'd always enjoyed its earthy smell and the way its leaves rustled.

As a kid, he'd spent many an hour daydreaming in the treehouse he built in the tree when he was ten years old. It was still there, although a board or two blew off every now and then when the wind got to howling.

He surveyed the homestead, what he could see of the six-hundred-and-forty acres. It wasn't large, but it was his and, when it came down to it, just right for him. He could keep up with his place and pull a paycheck over at the Whispering Pines, too. His grandparents had left the ranch to his mother, their only living child, and she'd willed it to him, her only child. Like his parents, he'd had just one child, who…

Cyrus tapped ashes from the tip of the cigarette into the ashtray and picked up the beer. He wasn't going down that dark alley tonight. After two swigs, he put the bottle down and commenced rocking. The porch floor boards creaked a duet with the worn wooden rocker.

For years, they'd had two adult-size rocking chairs on the porch plus a smaller one for Susan. Summer evenings, the three of them would rock and talk, rock and talk. Sometimes they'd eat brownies and homemade vanilla ice cream. Sometimes they'd have watermelon-seed spittin' contests. Sometimes they'd sit on the steps and count shooting stars.

No matter what the kid thought these days, her early years were good years. Every now and again as they sat together on the porch, she'd ask how he and her mom met and courted—and married. When his version didn't match with her mom's, Susan would laugh and laugh.

Despite the Pollyanna spin Helen put on the story, the fact was, they'd had a rocky start from the get-go. Cyrus grunted. Well, not the get-go. They'd been closer than cousins in elementary school, junior high and most of high school. At least he thought so.

Cyrus sucked at the cigarette again, coughed and dropped it in the ashtray. August second. The day—and how the smell of Helen's vanilla-scented hair filled the cab of his pickup—were as clear in his head as if time had no power to dull the memory. That was the day he left home the first time, a month before he would have started his senior year of high school.

Winds of Hope

❧

The night before, his girlfriend from the fifth grade through junior high and high school, the girl he planned to marry the day they graduated, had told him she wanted to date other boys their senior year. "It's not that I don't love you," Helen had said.

Slumped against the seatback of his old Ford pickup, his arm across her shoulders, he'd bent his head to peer into her eyes. "What?"

She focused on her hands. "It's that I've never dated anyone else, Cy. My mom says I should have that experience before we get married, just so...just so I'll be sure." Shifting, she faced him. "I don't want to marry anyone unless I'm one-hundred percent sure."

"Are you pullin' my leg?" Cyrus lowered his arm and twisted to see her better in the muted light from her parents' porchlight. "Cuz if you are, I don't think it's funny."

"I'm serious, Cy." Her voice was soft. She touched his shoulder.

He jerked away. "I'm one-hundred percent sure—two-hundred percent sure, and I have been since the day your family moved to the valley."

"I know."

"That isn't enough?"

"It takes two fully committed people to have a good marriage. That's what I want, a good marriage—when I'm older. Mom says we're too young to get married."

"So I'm not good enough for you?"

"I didn't say that."

He gripped the steering wheel with both hands, unable to comprehend life without Helen. Unwilling to comprehend life without Helen.

"Cy…" she whispered. "Please try to understand. We'll still be friends. Good friends, forever."

"Out!" He snarled at her. "Get out of my truck! If that's how you feel about me, about us, then there ain't nothin' more to talk about."

"But…"

Cyrus flung open the door, jumped out of the pickup and ran around to the passenger side. He yanked the door, nearly ripping it off its squawking hinges, and pulled her out of the truck. "It's over, Helen. We're done. Now get on in the house. Your mama is waitin' for her baby girl."

"Please, Cy—"

He slammed the door, marched to the driver's side, got in and wrenched the door shut.

She pounded on the window, but he hit the gas, spinning a U-turn on the wide graveled driveway. The pickup's back end swerved and rocked the truck, but he wound out of the turn and shot down the drive to the road, fully aware the truck tires spit rocks at Helen and billowed a dirt cloud in her face. He didn't care. She deserved it.

ॐ

The sun had not yet risen over the eastern wall of the canyon when Cyrus opened the pickup door to throw a box of clothes on the passenger seat. For a long moment, he stared at the dim spot where Helen had ridden ever since he bought the truck. With a shake of his head, he closed the door and went around to the driver's side.

He'd kissed his mom goodbye last night. But he hadn't told his dad he was leaving. He wanted to get on the road before his father awakened.

On his way into town to fill the gas tank, he passed his best friend's place. The barn door was open and he saw a light on inside. Larry was already milking cows. Most days, Cyrus would have stopped to chew the fat, as his grandpa liked to say, but not this morning. He was too choked up to talk. The vanilla aroma that lingered in the cab wasn't helping matters.

Losing Helen drilled a hole to the very core of his gut and filled it with unspeakable pain. The agony that clamped his midsection had wrung all the words out of his brain. If he tried to talk, he'd probably bawl like an orphan calf. Larry wouldn't know what to do with him.

Last night, after Helen dropped the bomb that would forever change his life, he'd driven the county's dirt roads for hours. When he was too worn out to see straight, he'd gone home to find his father deep in a drunken, snoring slumber on the couch in front of a television blasting an ad for used cars. He'd tiptoed past him to his parents'

57

bedroom, tapped the doorjamb and whispered, "Mom, you awake?"

He heard rustling and then her voice, soft. "Come in and close the door." Somehow, she knew he didn't want to include his father in the conversation. But then, he never wanted to include his father.

By the yard light sifting through the curtain, he could see she was sitting up. She patted the comforter. "Sit down."

He sat, smelling the night cream she slathered on every evening to protect her skin from the rigors of ranch life.

"What is it, son?"

He hadn't planned to tell her about Helen. All he'd intended to say was that he was going to Uncle Ted's place to work for him and that she should go with him and leave Dad to fend for himself. His uncle, whose cattle operation was much bigger than his father's, had told Cyrus many a time he'd hire him on his crew whenever he needed a change, no questions asked. Of course, he'd said those words on the sly, knowing his alcoholic brother would be mad as a swatted hornet by the loss of free labor.

Cyrus hadn't planned to cry, either, but the tears leaked out anyway. Swiping at his cheeks with the backs of his hands, he mumbled, "Helen's mom says…" His voice broke. "She says we're too young to be talkin' marriage. But—"

His mother squeezed his arm. "Edna is right, you know." Her voice was gentle. "You're both young, with years of living ahead of you. Why rush into marriage?"

"Because," he blurted, "because someone else might steal Helen."

She smiled. "I love Helen and I believe you two are a good match for each other. If you're destined for marriage, you'll come together again, after you've had time to mature."

"I can't stand to watch her with other guys, while I sit in the corner like a dunce."

"You don't have to sit in the corner. You can date other girls, be friends with them, have fun."

"I know every girl in the county. None of them holds a candle to Helen. She's the only one I want to date."

His mother sighed. "You can be so hardheaded sometimes, Cyrus."

"Come with me, Mom. Uncle Ted and Aunt Betty will let us both live there. Their house is big, plus Jeannie and John moved out after high school. I know Dad'll blow up, but he—"

"I can't leave your father, son. This ranch would fall to pieces if he was left on his own."

"That's okay. We don't need this old place. Dad and the ranch can nosedive into whatever hole he digs for himself."

"It is not okay, Cyrus Moore."

Cyrus blinked and jerked back. He hadn't heard that tone from her since she caught him practicing his slingshot aim on the chickens when he was nine.

"This was my grandparents' homestead," she said, her voice firm as a schoolteacher's, "all six-hundred and forty acres. It's not much, but it's mine and all I have to give you for an inheritance."

He squinted through the darkness at her. The wind shifted and the lace pattern ruffled across her face. "You mean, Dad isn't…"

"I mean, my father only agreed to my marriage to your father when I promised to keep the ranch in my name only. He knew better than I did what I was getting into, but I couldn't see beyond your dad's blue eyes. He has badgered me ever since to add his name to the title.

"You've probably heard some of our fights when he gets to thinking about it." She brushed hair from her forehead. "I've put up with a lot of guff from him over the years, but I refuse to back down on my promise to my father. Your father would sell the ranch out from under us for just one more bottle of whiskey."

Cyrus grunted, pulled a bandana from his back pocket and blew his nose. He didn't doubt that for one snap of a finger. Last month, his dad had sold the tractor that was only a couple years old, saying they needed to buy one with a cab on it. In the meantime, he'd get the old tractor behind the barn running again. According to his mother, the money had never made it to their bank account. And the old tractor still sat where it had sat for years, a forest of weeds growing up around it.

"This is my ranch, Cyrus, and yours. Your name is on the will. If I leave, the taxes won't get paid, the barn will fall down, mice will overrun the house and my grandparents' homestead will be taken from us and sold to someone else."

Cyrus stood and walked to the window. He'd known his grandparents homesteaded the property, but he hadn't known it was his mom's place and not his dad's. That changed everything. Neither parent had ever mentioned him being the heir, probably because it was a sore point between them.

He'd always assumed he'd inherit the ranch, but he hadn't thought much about it because it would be a long time in coming. Even so, he couldn't leave now. He turned from the window. "I'll stay, Mom, to help keep things going. But I won't go to school."

"Yes, you will."

"I can't."

"Are you using this as an excuse to get out of school, because if you are—"

"I told you. I can't watch Helen flirt with other yahoos in class or at lunch or at a ballgame. I'd lose my cool and deck 'em. Then I'd get kicked out of school. Count on it."

"Your dad acts worthless because he didn't finish high school and he thinks everyone looks down on him."

"Dad acts worthless because he's a drunk."

She blew out a long breath. "Your Uncle Ted is a firm believer in education. If you go to Colorado, he'll insist you finish school."

"That's okay by me. I just don't want to go to the same school as Helen." His uncle had promised him free room and board. He'd also told him he could work part-time when school was in session plus play sports, which his dad insisted was a "blasted waste of time." The real reason,

61

Cyrus knew, was that sports would take him away from the chores his father didn't want to do.

"Then go to Colorado."

"I can't leave you to… I shouldn't have mentioned it, Mom. You and Dad aren't able to work this place without me."

"I'll hire part-time help."

"I thought money was tight."

"It is, but I have a bit of a stash."

"I'll mail my paychecks home."

"You don't—"

"I will."

"I can't let you do that. Your father will drink your earnings dry."

"I'll send it to an account in town only you know about."

She shook her head.

He sat beside her again. "I thought I was the future owner."

"Yes, but…"

"Then let me help. You'll need to buy feed, bring the vet out now and then, pay taxes—everything it takes to keep this place in operation. If you don't let me help, I won't leave." He knew that meant he'd butt heads with his old man again and again, but he had to do what he had to do.

His mom leaned close to hug him. "I'll miss you, son, and I'll pray for your heart to heal." She kissed his cheek.

"I can't wait to see you graduate. What a grand, happy day that will be."

Cyrus stood. She would watch him graduate, he was sure of that, but his heart would never heal. Helen had shattered it beyond repair.

Winds of Hope

~

Life was good on his uncle's ranch. Plenty of food on the table, a beautiful setting with a mountain backdrop, a kind uncle and a sweet aunt. Best of all, he had satisfying work, the type that left him so tired he dropped into a dreamless slumber every night, with only a fleeting thought of Helen before he fell asleep.

He'd always expected to graduate from Copperville High School, but Rangeview High was all right. The teachers were downright decent folks and, for the most part, so were the students. Yeah, there was the class beefhead, but he paid the son of a gun no mind.

He'd wondered what to expect the first day, being the new kid in a small school in a small town where everyone knew everyone. Of course, word got out pronto, even before school started, that he was living with his aunt and uncle. He'd met some of the kids at the rodeo during the county fair, where he'd placed in calf roping and barrel racing and had taken first place in bronc riding. As a result, he'd gained admirers, including several girls, who made him feel part of the ranch crowd at school. But none of the gals, nice as they were, measured up to Helen.

Although everyone was friendly, the town kids and the ranch kids had distinctly different interests. The town kids might babysit after school or work at the library or the gas station, while Cyrus and his friends drove their pickups or rode the bus home to feed cattle, muck stalls and milk cows.

But everyone came together for sports. The entire community stood behind the team, whether it was football, basketball, wrestling or track—or baseball in the summer, a sport they didn't have in Copperville. Cyrus hadn't participated in baseball because he'd arrived at the ranch just a month before school started. Plus, Uncle Ted had put him to work right away. He discovered later that none of the ranch boys carved time out of busy summer obligations to play baseball. That was a sport for town kids.

In the few short weeks before school began, Cyrus learned the ropes of the ranch and got to know the other ranch hands. He helped move livestock down from the mountain pastures, baled and stacked hay, helped fence a new pasture and took over the training of his uncle's Arabian gelding, a colt named Ferdinand. Ted's border collie, Bart, a fleetfooted herd dog, followed him everywhere.

He went out for both football and basketball and was placed on the B squad, mostly due to his lack of experience. However, he was quick on his feet and a fast learner. The coaches played him often.

Whether on the bench or on the field or the gymnasium floor, he had a good time. His only regret was that his parents and Helen weren't in the stands cheering him on, something Ted voiced for him after they'd won a basketball game by three points.

His hand on Cyrus's shoulder, Ted had said, "That was a great play in the third quarter, Cy. Too bad your mom and dad weren't here to see it."

Cyrus had only grunted then, not wanting to show how much his parents' absence hurt. But now, sitting on his front porch, he took a swig of beer and sat back in his rocking chair. Reliving his moment of glory, he recalled the fancy footwork that had positioned him between taller opponents to score for Rangeview, a basket that turned the game in their favor.

He'd gone home during the holiday break, much to his mom's delight. His dad didn't have much to say to him, but he'd at least been sober on Christmas Day. New Year's Eve was a different story, a bender to beat all benders.

His mother's face was drawn and thin, yet she insisted she was fine. He did all the chores while he was home, so she could rest. Driving into town to pick up groceries for her, he'd seen Helen in a car with other smiling, laughing kids. He couldn't tell if she was holding hands with the guy next to her. She didn't see him and he didn't honk.

Winds of Hope

Shortly after supper a week before graduation, the house phone rang. Cyrus, who was sitting on the couch watching a wrestling match on television, heard his uncle answer the telephone. Moments later, he said, "Cy, your dad wants to yack at you."

Cyrus got up to walk over to the phone. His heart thumped and he could smell his armpits. His father had not called him since he left the ranch. Did this have something to do with his graduation? Were his parents not coming? He'd grudgingly admitted to himself that he missed his dad as well as his mom and had looked forward to seeing both of them.

Sounding more sober than Cyrus remembered him sounding in a long time, his dad said, "Hello, son. How are you?"

"Hi, Dad. I'm doing okay. How about you?"

"I've been better."

After a long pause Cyrus didn't know how to fill, his father said, "I'm doing all right, but your mom isn't so good."

Cyrus's chest clutched, as if squeezed by a giant fist. "What do you mean? Is Mom sick?"

"Yeah, came on sudden like. At first, we thought she had the flu, but it got worse and worse, so I finally took her to the doctor. She's got some sort of disease. Can't remember the name."

"Did he give her medicine?"

"He sent her straight to the hospital, and she's…well, like I said, she's not doing too good."

Heat rose from Cyrus's chest into his neck and face. "When did all this happen?" Dad ignoring the ranch needs was one thing, but ignoring his mom's needs was another. Good thing he wasn't there. He'd grab him by his scrawny neck and throw him against a wall.

"I wanted to call you earlier, but on the way to the hospital, your mother said, "Now, don't you go telling Cyrus. He'll think he has to come home. He needs to stay in Colorado and finish high school." He paused. "Truth be told, we both thought she'd get better. Your mom always pushes through, but the doc says she's too weak and wore out to fight off whatever this is."

Yeah, 'cause I left and you worked her to death. His mother had hired help like they'd talked about, but his father ran off one part-timer after another. Cyrus grimaced. No matter how much he blamed his dad, the fault ultimately lay with him. He should have stayed home where he belonged.

"Is she…?" Cyrus couldn't say the word.

"Yeah, son." His dad blew out a long, low breath. "The docs say your mom's not long for this world."

"I'm comin' home tonight."

"What about your graduation? She wanted to see you walk across that stage in the worst way."

70

And Cyrus had wanted to see her in the audience seated with his dad and Aunt Betty and Uncle Ted in the worst way. "I passed all my classes. That's all that matters. I'll throw my stuff in the truck as soon as I hang up and be there before sunrise."

"She'll be mighty pleased to see you."

Cyrus set the phone down. Maybe the doctors were wrong. They made mistakes, just like everyone else. Whether they were right or wrong, he needed to get home pronto—right after he said goodbye to Ferdinand and Bart.

Winds of Hope

❦

Seated on a hard metal folding chair at the front of the Grange Hall meeting room, Cyrus was certain Helen and her parents, Edna and Vern Linder, were seated behind him. The room overflowed with friends who'd known and loved his mom. But like a magnet, his former girlfriend tugged at his heart. Gripping the seat edge, he fought the urge to scan the crowd. As angry as he was right now about his mom's death, if he saw Helen with another guy, he'd probably knock his teeth out.

The death certificate, which he'd found in the mailbox that morning, stated the cause of his mother's demise as Hantavirus Pulmonary Syndrome. Every rancher in the West knew HPS was a severe respiratory disease that came from contact with rodent urine and droppings.

He'd questioned his dad, whose memory was fuzzy, but who thought his mom had mucked out the stalls in the barn just before she got sick. Two old horses his dad wouldn't give up spent their nights in the stalls. Cyrus wasn't sure if he was angrier with his father or with himself for allowing his mother to die.

Seated between his dad and Aunt Betty, Cyrus couldn't watch the preacher, who spoke at length about his mother's sweet spirit and kind deeds. Instead, he anchored his elbows on his knees, clasped his hands, balanced his chin on his knuckles—and glared at the floor.

From the pastor's words, the man appeared to know her well, which was no surprise. She'd attended his small church for years. Cyrus and his father accompanied her at

Christmas and Easter, but that was all. He wondered if the man knew what his mom had suffered at the hands of her husband.

The preacher had helped them plan the funeral proceedings, from beginning to end. But when it came to after-service greetings, his dad had insisted, "We don't need to do no lineup." They could talk with folks at the meal their neighbors provided in the hall. Cyrus was relieved he didn't have to endure a gauntlet of hugs and handshakes, especially from Helen and her parents.

But lunch was different. He couldn't avoid them there. He was about to take a bite of green-bean casserole when she leaned over his shoulder, her hair brushing his jaw. He knew it was Helen by the touch of her hand and her vanilla scent. He'd recognize that aroma anywhere.

"I loved your mom," she whispered. "She treated me like a daughter. And I'm still your forever friend, Cy, whether you like it or not."

He turned his head and she was replaced by her mother, who squeezed his shoulders and kissed his cheek. "I miss your mom already. She was a dear, dear friend."

He stood and said the only words he could manage, words of gratitude he'd heard his uncle say many times. "Thanks a million."

Helen's dad, Vern, shook his hand. "I miss your beat-up hat hanging on the rack by the front door, cowboy. If you need anything, let us know. You're welcome to come by the house anytime."

Cyrus nodded and focused on the couple waiting behind them.

Cyrus spent the summer repairing and restoring his grandparents' homestead, now his place, something neither he nor his dad mentioned. He fixed a broken windmill, mended trampled fences, had the vet out to treat a cow with a snakebite wound on its face and to test their few remaining cattle for disease. He cleaned the house, repaired the roof and shoveled out the barn—without wearing a mask. Whether he lived or died was of no consequence to him.

He also bought five yearlings to add to their small herd and warned his dad against trying to sell them. In return, his father told him to keep his hands off the horses. Cyrus's suggestion that they give the pair away or sell them to a slaughterhouse had not been well received.

On the one hand, hard work helped Cyrus focus on something other than his mom and Helen. On the other hand, it provided long, uninterrupted hours to think about the two most important women in his life. He told himself he needed to get a hobby, or maybe a horse like Ferdinand to train and a dog like Bart. But his dad and dogs were a bad combination, especially when alcohol was involved.

Helen had called, twice. Before he could hang up the first time, she'd asked him to meet her at Grandma's Cafe´ for a root beer float. She knew he loved root beer floats. But he wasn't about to sit across from her in public, where people could watch him fall to pieces. He told her he was busy. He had a ranch to run.

She tried to argue, but he said, "Gotta go," and hung up the phone. Two days later, a note from her arrived in the mail. All she'd written inside was, Forever Friends.

He tore the paper into tiny pieces. He didn't want to be Helen's friend. He wanted to be her husband.

She called another time to invite him to the lake for a trout fry with former classmates, a mini reunion of sorts, she said.

Yeah, that's just what he wanted to see, Helen snuggled up to some bozo. Besides, thanks to her, he had to finish school in Colorado. He hadn't been able to graduate from Copperville High, like she did.

He told her the same thing. "I'm busy. I've got a ranch to run." And she mailed him the same message. Forever Friends. This time, he burned the note.

His dad, who'd gone back to drinking shortly after the funeral, ignored Cyrus's cleanup campaign until the day Cyrus borrowed the neighbor's dump truck. He filled it with broken equipment, rolls of rusted wire, busted fence posts and miscellaneous other junk, including his dad's worn-out recliner and the stained, lumpy couch.

"You leave for a few months," his dad said, "and you come back all high and mighty, thinkin' you can make this place look like Ted's blasted palace on the hill."

"I'll buy you a new television and a better chair, Dad, one that doesn't smell like booze. It's trash."

"That's for me to decide."

Cyrus tossed one last piece of scrap metal, a tarnished, bent bicycle frame he didn't recognize, in the back of the big truck and climbed into the cab. "I decided for you."

His dad threw the beer bottle he'd just emptied at the truck.

"This is Norm's truck," Cyrus said.

"I don't give a—"

Shaking his head, Cyrus started the engine. You son of a gun. He leaned out the window. "Meant to tell you. Uncle Ted wants you to call him."

"What for?"

"Just call him." Uncle Ted had told Cyrus that anytime his dad got out of hand, he should tell him to call. He'd give him what-for.

Cyrus didn't know whether his dad had phoned Ted or not, but he hadn't offered to help unload the new furniture. And then he'd bellyached every day, all day, about how uncomfortable the chair and couch were and that the television was too bright. When Cyrus told him to give it time, he'd get used to the changes, he'd promptly poured whiskey on the chair seat and sat in it.

A smirk on his face, he gazed straight at Cyrus. "By golly, it is better. Just like the old one."

That's when Cyrus knew the two of them would not survive cooped up in the house together through the winter. He called his uncle and told him he'd like to hire on again, if he'd have him. The thought of his dad destroying all he'd fixed over the summer pained him, but Norm Bainter, the neighbor who'd helped him clean up the place, agreed to continue working part-time. The man had learned to ignore his dad's rants, get the work done and go home, leaving him alone with his bottle.

For a second time, Cyrus left home.

Winds of Hope

✑

He stood up from the rocker, stretched his back and began to pace the porch. Slick also got to his feet. The dog squeezed between the rails. A moment later, he was chasing a wayward chicken back to the coop.

Those were hard days. Cyrus rubbed his jaw. Unsettled and aimless, he was like a boxcar hobo in a Ford pickup. He hadn't stayed long with his aunt and uncle. The yearning for his mom and Helen and home, a home he couldn't return to, was too strong.

Winds of Hope

❧

He'd drifted from state to state and ranch to ranch. Hard work kept his mind from wandering, most of the time. Too often, he wished he could call his mother or send her pictures. She'd had a great love for the West, and he'd gained a deeper appreciation for the region's open spaces, rugged mountains and boundless beauty.

His basic needs for food and shelter were met wherever he worked, so the bulk of his paychecks landed in the Copperville bank account. Once in a great while, he invested in a new pair of Levis or work boots and sometimes he took in a show, if the nearest town had a movie theater.

Mostly, he spent his free time driving around in his truck or reading the paperback westerns and detective novels the ranchers left in the bunkhouses. But if the books had romance in them, he threw them against a wall and went to bed.

About the time he thought he'd come to terms with life minus his mom and Helen, his dad died. Norm found him crumpled in the weeds between the old tractor and the barn wall, a whiskey bottle clutched in his unyielding fingers and a pool of congealed blood beneath his head. He'd landed on a rusted shovel blade. The coroner hadn't bothered with an autopsy.

Cyrus was about to bury his father without ceremony when his mother's pastor volunteered to officiate a service and the neighbor lady offered to arrange lunch at the Grange Hall. Once again, he sat with his elbows on his knees, his chin on his knuckles, and his gaze on the floor. Aunt Betty sat on one side of him and Uncle Ted on the other. Despite their presence, he felt alone, more alone than ever before.

While the preacher struggled to find kind words to say about his father, mostly using stories from the long-gone days before he succumbed to alcohol's stranglehold, Cyrus's mind oscillated between two thoughts—he was on his own now, and he had a ranch to run.

He'd been working in Montana when Norm called to tell him about his dad. The Montana job was a good one. The ranch owner paid well and treated his ranch hands with respect. Cyrus would have liked to return there. But he had a responsibility to honor his heritage and his mother by caring for the house and barn her parents built and the land they'd worked so hard to "prove up."

He'd checked out the Homestead Act, which he'd probably studied in Wyoming History class. If he'd known about his mother's promise to her father back then, he might have paid more attention. At a library in Montana, he'd learned that in order to "prove up," or secure ownership of homesteaded land, an applicant had to build a house, grow crops, make improvements to the land and live on it for five years. Evidently his grandparents had met all the requirements.

The preacher had barely said "amen" when Helen's parents were at his side. Edna hugged him, the scent of his mother's brand of cold cream on her cheek. "I'm so sorry, Cyrus," she said. "Seems your mother, bless her soul, just departed this earth, and now your dad is gone. Will you be returning to your home place?"

"Yeah…" Cyrus shrugged. "Guess I will." He didn't mention how difficult settling down would be for him after all his wanderings, especially with his mother's absence from the house—and Helen nearby. And he hadn't forgotten that Edna was the one who told Helen to break off their relationship.

She wiped a tear from her cheek. "Helen sends her sympathy. She'd be here today, but she's in the midst of final exams at nursing school in Scottsbluff."

"Tell her thanks a million for me." He tried to smile. This was the first he'd heard that Helen was going to school in Nebraska. Seems he would have heard the scuttlebutt by now. But then, he hadn't been around.

She'd talked often about becoming a nurse. However, he'd been too bent on marriage to acknowledge her interests. If they'd married right out of high school, he'd have stood in her way, like his dad stood in his mom's way and kept her from becoming a teacher. Maybe that's why she taught Sunday school year after year.

Helen's dad, Vern, clapped him on the shoulder. "We're here for you, son. Whatever you need. I'll help out any way I can and be glad to loan you equipment. Just say the word and I'll stop by with my hammer to shore up your barn. A strong wind could knock it clean over."

"I'd love to fix you a home-cooked meal now and then," Edna added. "And help you get your house in order. In fact, if you don't mind, I'd like to clean your house. I doubt your dad was much of a housekeeper."

That was an understatement. His mom would be appalled at the condition of their home and the yard—and the barn. "That's real nice of you, but you don't—"

"I want to, not just for you, but for your mother's sake." Another tear trickled down her cheek. "Her grandparents' homestead meant the world to her."

She'd read his mind.

"Well, yeah…"

"I'll be there first thing Monday."

Edna showed up early Monday morning, like she promised, and so did most of their neighbors and many of the townspeople, including Larry, who was on leave from the Army. They brought with them Norm's dump truck, a backhoe, pickups, tractors, mowers, rakes, shovels, wheelbarrows, brooms, mops, cleaning supplies, sponges, rags and more. And food—lots of food.

They were such a happy crew and so eager to assist him, Cyrus couldn't help but smile as he worked side-by-side with friends he'd known from birth. He even responded to their sympathetic words and handshakes with gratitude rather than grumpiness. His only sour moment came when he found two women scrubbing the couch and chair he'd bought for his dad. Their faces were scrunched as if they were trying not to breathe.

"Stop that!" The words came out harsher than he'd expected.

Their heads popped up, and he caught their startled expressions.

"I mean…" He softened his tone. "They're booze-soaked and worthless. I'll ask a couple of the guys to help me throw them in the dump truck."

The women sat back, their relief obvious.

"We have a set out in the garage that my parents left behind when they passed," said a woman who was washing the picture window. "Two chairs and a sofa. All three pieces are in great shape. You can have them, if you'd like."

By the time all was said and done, Cyrus not only had new living room furniture, some kind soul had replaced the mattress and box springs in his parents' bedroom. The crew hadn't just given his place a lick and a promise, they'd scrubbed the carpets, painted the walls, and scoured the kitchen and bathroom from floor to ceiling.

Every single person dug in with enthusiasm, and there was nothing shoddy about their work. They'd mowed and cleared debris from the yard and field in front of the house, got the old tractor chugging again, and repaired and cleaned the barn. Larry, good ol' Lar, offered to find homes for the horses. On top of everything else, the women packed his freezer and refrigerator to the brim with food. He didn't have to cook for a long, long time.

Winds of Hope

Dusk settled quickly once the final wedge of sunshine slipped behind the canyon wall. Cyrus watched a flock of birds swoop into the cottonwoods by the creek and commence chattering. He wondered if they were making plans for the next day before slumber overtook them.

He stubbed out the cigarette in the black melamine ashtray his father had used and got to his feet, his knees cracking. For a moment, he stood on the top step, rubbing his lower back and staring at the darkening sky. Good people. The local folks were mighty good people.

Thinking back, he remembered how often this neighbor or that friend just happened to be driving by after his dad's death and stopped at the house to say hello. He wondered if they'd charted a schedule to make sure he didn't go too many days without someone checking on him. They must have known Norm came over every so often to help him get the ranch up and running again. But the company was nice and a steady flow of visitors kept him from sinking into a quicksand of loneliness and grief.

He'd said farewell to nary a one of them when he left. Yet, the community welcomed him back with open arms. Both times he took off, he was in an all-fired hurry to break away, too bloomin' riled up to hang around a moment longer. Now, he was glad to be home.

An encounter with Helen was inevitable. He dreaded the first meeting. Even so, he was ready to accept her as a friend and nothing more—or at least he thought he was.

Cyrus chuckled and trod the remaining three steps to the path that connected with the outbuildings. He kicked Slick's well-chewed baseball off the path. "Fetch, Slick." The dog took off after the ball, scrabbling behind a fence post to retrieve it.

The air chilled with the sun's drop behind the canyon rim. He rolled his shirtsleeves down and snapped the cuffs, remembering how meeting up with Helen came sooner than he expected. He started for the chicken coop, thinking that was another day he'd never forget. The morning was clear as crystal in his mind's eye.

∞

Frying pan in hand, he'd been digging through the pantry. What in blue blazes had happened to the dish rack that sat beside the sink for as long as he could remember? He didn't see it in the pantry and was about to search the cupboards one more time, when he heard a knock on the front door. Striding across the living room, he opened the door wide.

Edna stood on the porch, a smile on her face and a dish rack in her hand.

He stared at the dish rack.

She stared at the frying pan.

He lowered the pan. Did the woman read everybody's minds—or just his?

"You might have noticed we tossed your dish rack."

"I was lookin' for it just now."

"It was…" She paused, apparently hunting for the right words. "Let's just say, unsafe." She held out the new one. "I hope you don't mind."

He reached for the rack, but she pulled back. "How about I take it and your pan into the kitchen, and you help Helen with the flowers."

Helen? He peered at the car parked in front of the house. And there she was, standing by the open trunk. She waved.

He handed the pan to Edna, who said, "Your mom's pansy patch is looking puny this year, which would have made her sad. I doubt your dad ever watered it."

Cyrus grunted. "The thought probably never entered his head." The only thing he'd seen his father water was the nearest tree after he'd drunk a couple beers. But he wasn't about to mention that to Helen's mother.

"In her honor and memory, I'd like to fill in the bare spots, if it's okay with you, that is."

He shrugged. "I can pay for the flowers."

"Oh, no. This is my treat, something tangible I can do to remember your sweet mother." She raised the pan and the rack. "I'll take these to the kitchen and then get busy planting. I'm thinking a mix of pansies on each side of the porch would be pretty." Without waiting for a response, she stepped past him into the living room.

He glanced at Helen, again. She wiggled her fingers, again. And he noticed two things. One, she appeared as nervous as he felt, and two, she was as pretty as ever. The early morning sun haloed her dark hair and her smile triggered a tornado in his chest.

Taking the porch steps one at a time, he walked toward the car. What could he say to her? *You're a sight for sore eyes? Long time no see? Good to see you, stranger?* All clichés, but the sight of her wiped any possibility of original thoughts from his brain. *Friends*, he reminded himself. From this point forward, they'd be friends—and nothing more.

When he stopped four feet in front of Helen, she seemed shorter. He must have grown some. Of course, the last two or three pairs of jeans he'd bought were a size longer as were the long-sleeved shirts he purchased at the same time.

He stuck his hands in his pockets. "I shouldn't have taken off from your place so gol durn fast that night. I was downright rude, nastier than a rabid skunk. I've wondered ever since if the rocks stirred up by my tires blasted you."

"No, Cy." Her eyes were as soft as her smile. "The only thing injured that night was my feelings. And, of course, your feelings, too."

"I've owed you an apology for almost three years." Cyrus cleared his throat. "It's high time to say I'm sorry." There. He'd done it. He was a day late and a dollar short, but he'd finally spit it out.

"I'm sorry, too. I appreciate your apology."

And then they'd stood there gazing at each other, pansy perfume drifting between them.

Finally, Cyrus said, "I hear congratulations are in order cuz you just graduated from nursing school in Nebraska. You plannin' to get a job there?"

She tilted her head. "Yes and no."

He lifted an eyebrow.

"I'll work in a doctor's office in Scottsbluff while I study to be a nurse practitioner."

"How's that different than being a plain ol' nurse?"

"A nurse practitioner can diagnose illness and prescribe remedies, something a nurse can't do. This area has been without a healthcare professional since Dr. Wilson died five years ago. I'm hoping to fill that gap, not to get rich, but to help our friends and neighbors. Sure, we have the EMTs who run the ambulance in town, but I'll have better training and be able to provide more services than they can."

"Will you take over Doc Wilson's office? It's still vacant."

"I think I'd rather go into homes. That would be more personal plus save the cost of an office building, utilities, a receptionist and all that."

He folded his arms. "How long will the extra schooling take you?"

"Two years, three with a residency."

"Oh." He tried to hide his disappointment. At first, he'd been afraid of running into her around town. Now, he wouldn't see her at all.

She stepped closer and grabbed him by the biceps. Shocked, he pulled back, but she held tight. "I've missed you, Cy. A lot."

"Well, yeah…" Head down, he shuffled the toe of his boot in the gravel, every cell in his body tingling with her touch. "I missed you, too."

"Can we be—?"

"Yeah, yeah. We can be friends, if that's what you want. But that won't matter much, cuz you won't be around." He tried not to sound bitter.

"I want to be more than friends."

He twisted his head toward her. "What?"

"I never stopped loving you."

"Are you joshing me?" He pulled from her grasp. "Cuz if you are, I don't—"

"That's what you said when..." Her brow puckered. "I was serious then, and I'm serious now. No doubts in my mind. You're the one for me, Cyrus Moore—if you'll have me."

He heard footsteps behind him and then the sound of Helen's mother clearing her throat.

"I hate to interrupt," she said, "but I could use some help carrying those starter trays over to the porch. I'd like to plant the flowers while the morning is still cool."

And so began the happiest—and sometimes the hardest—days of his life.

Winds of Hope

❧

With Slick's help, Cyrus shooed the last of the hens into the chicken coop, closed and locked the door. The only reason he kept chickens these days was to supply the WP's dining hall with eggs and, occasionally, chickens he butchered and plucked himself. He no longer raised cattle because he could get all the beef and bison meat he needed from Mike over at the WP.

He checked the barn for stray wildlife and closed the big door. He'd learned the hard way it was best not to lock a skunk or an angry raccoon in overnight. These days he kept his pickup in the barn rather than livestock. Calling to Slick, he headed for the house.

His dog normally slept in the barn, but a pack of coyotes had been roaming the area, killing calves. Cyrus wanted Slick in the house to warn him if they came close. His shotgun sat propped against the doorframe, loaded and ready for him to take aim the moment the dog growled.

Feeling chilled, he started a fire in the wood stove and settled in his recliner with the Laramie Boomerang, the newspaper that had come in the mail that day. He subscribed to several newspapers from southeast Wyoming and northeast Colorado towns. Radio and television news would be more up-to-date than two-day-old newspapers, but he enjoyed the columns and the local sports commentaries, something a man couldn't get on bloomin' national news.

Slick circled and circled and finally curled in the middle of the rug that anchored the center of the living room. Cyrus switched on the lamp beside his chair and opened the paper. But like his dog, his mind circled, always landing in the center of the few short years he'd had with Helen and their daughter, Susan.

Unable to focus on the words, he draped the newspaper across his legs and rested his head against the afghan Helen crocheted for the back of his chair. She'd never said why, but he had a feeling it had something to do with the grease spot that had formed there.

✐

The three years he'd waited for Helen to come home for good had been almost as tough as the previous three years. But this time he had phone calls and letters from her—and her constant assurance that she loved him. He begged her to marry him before she finished her schooling. But she insisted it wouldn't be right because they'd be forced to lead separate lives, her in Scottsbluff, and him on his ranch. Once they married, she wanted to be able to go home to him every night.

Sometimes she flew into Laramie for holidays and he picked her up at the airport. Sometimes he drove to Scottsbluff, where he'd bunk with a ranch hand he knew there. Sometimes they met in Cheyenne. They'd spend the day together then turn around late in the evening to drive lonely roads home.

Parting was always agony, for both of them. But Helen would hug him and say, "Thirteen more months, Cyrus. Just thirteen more months." And then, "Five-and-a-half more months, Cyrus." "Just eleven weeks, Cy. Mom and I have the wedding all planned. I can't wait for you to see my dress."

He would hold her close and say nothing. No matter the number of months or weeks, they all represented an eternity in his book. But he'd made it through the previous painful years without her. He'd suck it up and slog to the other end of this lonesome valley. Like the song said, he had to walk it by himself, even though Helen reminded him often that she walked alongside him now.

Finally, she returned home for good. A month later they married and Helen began to serve the community like she'd hoped to do. She sutured wounds, set broken bones, tended burns, delivered babies in the middle of the night, rode with her patients when Wyoming Life Flight transported them to regional hospitals. More than once, Cyrus had driven several hours to pick her up. But he didn't mind the opportunity to be alone with his wife.

He managed the ranch plus worked for the Whispering Pines Guest Ranch. At first, his intent was to be a good neighbor and help Laura and Dan Duncan get their ranch up and running. But then there was one more fence to build, one more hayfield to mow, one more cow to deworm or dehorn. And it wasn't long before the Duncans said they wanted to pay him for his labor and hired him as their first employee.

Helen was dedicated to her work, but she was also dedicated to her family. She joyed in caring for Cyrus and Susan, who was born eight years after their marriage. They laughed on the porch together, ate popcorn and told stories by the wood stove, and walked and talked along the trail he'd made through their property.

And then Helen got sick. Thinking she had the flu, she wore a mask and gloves when she entered other homes. But the muscle aches, dizziness, chills and abdominal pains wore on and on. The dark circles beneath her eyes grew darker while her cheeks grew paler.

Following a long night of coughing and labored breathing, she rolled toward Cyrus and rasped between coughs, "Maybe I should stay home today."

Cyrus smoothed her hair from her face. "You'll not only stay home, Nurse Moore, you'll stay in this bed and let Dr. Moore take care of you. Just tell me what you need and I'll get it for you."

Due to Helen's erratic schedule, she and Cyrus shared cooking duties. His mother had taught him to cook and his family loved her chicken soup recipe. First thing he did after he made a steam tent for Helen was cook up a big pot of soup.

But a day of rest and chicken soup didn't help. Helen coughed and wheezed so hard the next night that Cyrus cocooned her in quilts, put her in the backseat of her SUV and drove her the two hours to the Steamboat Springs hospital. The emergency-room staff lost no time hooking her to oxygen.

Cyrus watched, hanging at the fringe of the action, until a doctor sent him to the waiting room, where he paced the nearby hallway like a caged tiger, more frightened than he'd ever been in his life.

Winds of Hope

❧

Cyrus threw the newspaper aside and jumped up. Slick hopped to his feet and headed for the door. But instead of leaving the house, his master paced around the rug, into the kitchen and back again. The dog followed for a couple passes but finally settled on the rug and returned to sleep.

Cyrus, on the other hand, kept moving, haunted by the awful memories of the ten days Helen spent in the hospital, fighting for her life.

Winds of Hope

◢◣

His worst nightmare resurfaced when the doctor told them she suffered from the same illness that had killed his mother, Hantavirus Pulmonary Syndrome. Beside himself with frustration, he tore into her the moment the doctor left the room. "I told you and Susan to wear masks and gloves when you clean the barn!"

Susan, who was thirteen at the time, shoved him away from the bed. "Stop yelling at Mom! It's not her fault she's sick. She didn't clean the barn and neither did I."

He glared from Susan to Helen. "Then how in tarnation did this happen?"

"Come here, sweetie." Helen motioned Susan to her side and took her hand. She was about to speak again when she was overcome with a coughing fit.

Head bowed, he walked to the other side of the bed. When she quieted, he said, "I'm sorry. That was uncalled for."

"Actually, I did clean the barn," Helen rasped. "It was a beautiful, sunny day and a couple of my afternoon appointments were canceled." She coughed and Susan handed her a plastic cup with a straw.

After a sip, she continued. "You'd been so busy over at Laura and Dan's place, that I thought, 'What can I do to ease Cyrus's load around here?' The first thing that came to mind was the barn. I opened the big door to let the sunlight in, picked up a rake and went to work. Never once did I think of wearing a mask. It had been so many years since you even let me go near the barn."

Breathing hard, Cyrus clenched and unclenched his fists.

"I'm sorry, Cy," Helen whispered, "but what's done is done."

And she'd done it for *him*.

He left the hospital only to shower and shave at the motel—and then only when a friend or Susan was there to sit with Helen. But he didn't stay away long, convinced that by holding his wife's hand and whispering in her ear, he could infuse her with his strength and will her to live.

But his presence wasn't enough. On day ten, she revived long enough to kiss him and Susan goodbye and apologize because she couldn't hang on. She had to go. And then she closed her eyes and breathed one last shallow, labored, rattling breath.

Cyrus stopped to peer out the kitchen window. A quarter moon was rising above the trees. Loneliness wrapped his soul once again. The two of them had spent many an evening on the swing they kept out back, holding hands and watching the moon climb the night sky. They'd had twenty-one good years together, which didn't begin to be long enough.

He returned to the living room to toss another log into the stove.

From the moment Helen died, he and Susan had floundered like a couple of trout on a creek bank, neither of them knowing how to act without their anchor. Helen had been the center of their home and of their lives. Like two planets, they'd revolved around their sun, Helen. But when her light faded and she no longer moored their solar system, they drifted apart from each other.

On the rare occasions they happened to cross paths, they collided and knocked chunks out of each other's crusts. Leaving empty, blistered craters behind, they'd ricochet off to separate galaxies, her schooling and his work.

Susan loved school and despite her grief, maintained straight A's. Her friends said she studied too much, but Cyrus knew homework was her salvation. The girl had lost both parents—her mother to death and her father to despair and depression.

Cyrus sunk into his chair. He could see all that now. But back then, dealing with a grieving teenage girl on top of his own heartache was more than he could handle. All he could see was an out-of-control, mouthy brat. The two of them had one knock-down, drag-out squabble after another. Yeah, he'd gotten a little testy and cantankerous now and then, but he never laid a hand on her.

⊷

And then Susan began avoiding him. Some kids would have turned to drinking or drugs or run off. Not Susan. She dug deeper into the books, leaving her bedroom to eat and shower only when he was gone or in bed.

At least, he thought she ate. She was skinnier than a rail and didn't make much of a dent in the meager refrigerator contents. He should have shopped more often, but buying groceries by himself was like chopping through briars. Too hard, just too dagblasted hard.

They both would have shriveled up and died if it hadn't been for Edna, who came by every now and then to stock the refrigerator. She also made sure Susan had school clothes and a prom dress. The two were as close as a cow and her calf.

In spite of her love for her grandmother, Susan left town the day after she graduated from high school. He knew she'd gotten a full-ride scholarship to Harvard, and she informed her grandmother when she was about to graduate four years later. But she said she didn't plan to walk the stage to get her diploma. No need for anyone to drive all the way across the country for the ceremony.

From Edna, he learned his daughter accepted a research position at a highly acclaimed aquatic ecology laboratory in San Diego. What in tarnation anyone did at an aquatic ecology laboratory was beyond him. But, whatever cranked her engine...

His updates concerning Susan's whereabouts came to a halt the day Edna and Vern were killed in a car accident.

The driver who'd been following behind them on icy roads reported that Vern apparently swerved to avoid a deer running across the mountain highway. The pickup had tumbled end over end and hit a tree part way down the steep incline, killing them both instantly. Their deaths shook the community and Cyrus to the core. Edna and Vern had come as close to replacing his parents as anyone could.

Susan returned home for her grandparents' double funeral. She even stayed in her old bedroom. Cyrus remembered the shock of seeing her for the first time in… He wasn't sure how many years. A backpack on one shoulder, she'd tromped into the house in hiking boots.

Her dark hair was long and straight and clasped at the base of her neck. She wore a black shirt, black pants and a big black watch on her left arm. Considering she'd come from California, her cheeks didn't appear to have been touched by sunshine. They were as pale as a dishtowel. Her mother and grandmother would have suggested she add color to her wardrobe—and to her face. Cyrus said nothing.

With barely a hello and a hug, Susan stuck her nose in the air and sniffed. "Something stinks in here, Dad."

"Yeah, well, I got kinda backed up—"

She marched toward the kitchen. "Did Grandma clean this house for you after I left?"

"Couldn't stop her."

Standing in the kitchen doorway, eyeing him in his easy chair, she placed a hand on her hip. "As if you tried."

"I did."

"You'll have trouble finding someone else to work for free in this podunk town."

"Your grandmother didn't work for free."

"I never saw you pay her."

It took everything within him not to launch out of the chair, grab her and throw her over his knee for a good paddlin'. That would knock her cocky attitude down a few notches. "Ever since your mom died, I've been paying the Cut, Curl & Comb for your grandmother's weekly appointments."

Before his daughter could say something else snooty, he added, "Plus a hefty tip. Linda Sue always smiles real big when she sees me walkin' in the door."

Susan shrugged and spoke very little from that point forward. But when she did talk to him, which didn't happen often, she wore a smirk he longed to wipe off her face.

The two cousins who inherited their grandparents' property along with Susan lived out of state, like she did. None of the three had a desire to return to Wyoming, so they leased the land to a neighboring farmer and rented the house to a young family.

Cyrus was galled to no end that not one of them chose to keep the ranch operating under the family name. But if they didn't have a hankering for that kind of work, it was probably best they didn't try to make a go of it. He wondered if Susan would do the same with his grandparents' homestead.

The thought aggravated him so much he considered bulldozing the house and barn so no outsiders could live there. At the height of his vexation, he contemplated selling the whole kit and caboodle and riding the circuit, cowpunching again. But he'd promised his mother he wouldn't let his dad hound him into sharing ownership and that he'd pass the homestead on to his children.

Maybe his daughter, his only heir, would marry someday and decide to return home to raise a family. But it was no skin off his nose. He'd be buried six-foot under, no matter what she wound up doing.

❧

Cyrus picked up the newspaper again. At this rate, he'd never get the cotton pickin' thing read. But the print blurred. He closed his weary eyes.

That was the last he'd seen of Susan. He was stumped by her bullheaded snobbery, and her mother would have been heartbroken. But maybe he deserved Susan's cold shoulder. At any rate, what was done was done. He needed to accept the fact she wanted nothing to do with him.

He clamped his jaw and rubbed his stubbled chin. Things would have been well and good if Laura at the WP hadn't gone off and hired that East Coast woman to fill Dan's spot in the office. Cyrus shook his head. Dan Duncan's death last fall was another loss that rocked Copperville and the surrounding farms and ranches. He was one of the good guys, the best of the best.

Just last week, he'd been ruminating about how Dan always had a smile and an encouraging word for everyone he came across. He was also quick to overlook an insult. If he was around, he'd be saying, "Let bygones be bygones, Cyrus. Get on with life." And he would be right. What was past was past, water under the bridge. Time to move on.

But then this morning Laura had shown him a sheet of paper with a picture at the top. "This is the young woman who's coming to do a three-month marketing internship here. Isn't it amazing how much she resembles Susan?"

Seeing someone who could have been Susan's sister jolted his heart like he'd stumbled into an electric fence. And recalling the picture just now sent a twister to his stomach. He frowned. He didn't mean to get down on his boss, but Laura knew his daughter didn't want anything to do with him.

"She recently graduated from a Pennsylvania university with a degree in marketing." Laura had smiled at him, her eyes bright. "If the internship goes okay, we'll keep her on staff—that is, if she's interested in staying on at the WP. Her name is Kate Neilson."

Cyrus glared at his living-room ceiling. Women with bloomin' college degrees from back east didn't set well with him. He folded the newspaper and switched off the lamp. A Harvard education had turned his daughter into a la-di-da smarty pants. This woman wouldn't be any different.

Dagnabit, why in tarnation did she have to look so much like Susan? He pushed himself out of the chair. Seeing her around the ranch day after day would be like a knife in the gut, stabbing and twisting, stabbing and twisting. Wasn't it enough he'd already been through the mill with women?

Cyrus opened the stove door and stirred the embers. If it wasn't for the Duncans counting on him to run the dining hall during the guest season, he'd take his leave of the Whispering Pines. He slammed the stove door, latched it and straightened, his hand on his back.

He'd have to buck up and face the changes at the WP like a man. But if that Neilson woman got uppity with him, he'd give her the dickens, no holds barred—a piece of his mind she'd wish he'd kept to himself.

MIKE

AT THE SOUND OF HIS two-way radio crackling to life, Mike Duncan, co-owner of the Whispering Pines Guest Ranch, flicked the reins and guided his horse, Lightning, around a snowdrift. He stopped on the far side of the temporary enclosure he and the crew had erected earlier that morning. Other than a couple drifts from the last storm, the trampled, brown grass within the makeshift corral was mostly bare of snow.

They'd used the corral panels he and Clint Barrett, the WP's foreman, built to create a good-sized branding trap at the base of the mountain pasture. The strategy was simple. All they'd had to do was square off a fence corner with the panels plus include a gate for easy access.

His dad had never used branding traps to make calf-branding easier and more efficient. But he and Clint were in charge now, and he was pleased with how well the panels functioned. He pulled off his fleece-lined leather gloves and stuffed them in a jacket pocket, thinking he wouldn't mention the panels to his mom. At least not yet. He wasn't sure she was ready to hear he'd veered from Dad's "tried-and-true" methods.

Mike slid the radio from his belt and pushed the button. "I'm here, Mom. Had to distance myself from an unhappy calf."

Two grunting men wrestled a squirming, bawling calf to the frozen ground and another lifted an ash-hot branding iron from a fire. Up the hill, Mike's big collie, Tramp, charged around cows, helping Clint cut another calf from the herd. Cattle mooed, Tramp barked, and Clint, swinging his rope, hollered, "Git over here."

In the summer, all the commotion that accompanied branding created a dust cloud. But this was late May, between spring snowstorms. The breath of men and animals alike misted the cool air and mingled with the smell of wood smoke, singed hair and fresh cow patties.

Laura Duncan came on the radio. "You still branding?"

"Almost done." She'd wanted him and Clint to get to the branding earlier, but the weather hadn't cooperated. Plus, they'd been busy fixing equipment and making other repairs to ready the ranch for the guest season.

"Are the calves in good shape?"

"Doing great." Mike surveyed the herd. "They've healed from the dehorning we did earlier."

"You still have some late-season calves to brand, right?" Without waiting for an answer, she said, "You know, your dad liked to finish all the branding before the guests arrived."

Mike let static rattle the airwaves before he responded. "Yeah, Mom, I remember." He didn't mention that he'd recently placed cattle decisions in Clint's hands. His own focus would be on the bison and on guest activities.

Lightning snorted and shook his head. Mike patted his horse's dark neck.

"I won't keep you," Laura said. "I just wanted to let you know I'm taking lunch over to Dymple. This is the last chance I have to spend time with her before our guest season begins. But I left some chili for you in the slow cooker, cornbread in the oven and a salad in the fridge. I also put butter out to soften for the cornbread."

Mike frowned. "Uh…thanks." He glanced at the other men, who appeared oblivious to his conversation with his mother, even though they each carried radios on their belts. He was grateful for the distractions and the noise that kept them from hearing his mom's detailed description of the lunch she'd prepared for him.

She knew he could cook—she'd taught him. And he'd taken care of himself just fine during the six years he spent at the university. But ever since Dad died, she seemed to find solace in feeding him food his father enjoyed. Chili and cornbread had been one of his favorite meals.

He depressed the talk button again. "Tell Dymple 'hi' from her favorite grandson." Though Dymple Forbes was not his grandmother, she'd called him her favorite grandson for years, which he considered an honor. A long-retired schoolteacher, Dymple was, in his book, the most unique woman in the Copperville area—and the wisest.

Laura laughed. "I'll be sure to tell her."

Dymple had been his third-grade teacher. He could still remember the day his mother walked him into Miss Forbes's classroom. Although she was a petite woman, she seemed to tower over him. And her bright gaze pierced right through his eyes into his brain, which frightened him so

115

much he could barely speak. He'd heard she was the strictest teacher in the school.

Finally, he managed to squeak out what his mother had told him to say. "Hello, Miss Forbes. My name is Michael Duncan. I'm happy to be in your class this year."

He knew he'd just told a whopper. He wasn't happy—he was scared to death. But then Dymple had smiled and reached to shake his hand. "Welcome, Mr. Duncan. I'm very happy to have you in my class. May I call you Mike?"

They'd been close ever since. He grinned. Dymple was still the livewire she'd been in her younger years. The single braid down her back was the same, although it was no longer brown. And she'd worn her signature denim jumpers with plaid shirts beneath and hiking boots below every day for as long as he could remember. Yep, one of a kind.

"I'd better get going," Laura said. "See you tonight."

Mike eyed the sky. Dark clouds were gathering on the horizon to the north. The brisk air smelled moist. He was about to warn her about the weather when she came on again. "I almost forgot. I meant to tell you what Dymple said earlier on the phone."

He waited. A hawk dived after its prey in the far distance.

"I told her I was taking chili and cornbread over to her house for lunch. She said..." Laura imitated Dymple's quavering voice. "'That sounds marvelous, dear. I've recently been craving your chili. You put just the right amount of sawdust in it.'"

He arched an eyebrow. Sawdust?

Laura chuckled. "I think she meant spices."

"That's a good one." Mike laughed. "The best yet. The aphasia she got when she hit her head on the tombstone is bad, but I sure get a kick out of her crazy words."

"Thought you'd enjoy her latest. Bye, Mike."

"Watch the road report, Mom. Clouds are building. The new storm they predicted is on the way." She'd been so sad since Dad died. He was glad she was spending the afternoon with Dymple, who could cheer the most sorrowful soul. But the roads would likely be slick by the time she drove home.

"Will do."

Mike clipped the radio to his belt, put on his gloves and headed Lightning to the gate, where he dismounted to open it. As soon as he did, Clint and Tramp shepherded an evasive brown-and-white calf into the corral, despite its best efforts to dodge them. Once they were inside, Mike closed the gate and Clint swung his lariat. The noose snaked along the ground, circling the calf's hind legs on the first try. He jerked the rope tight and the calf fell onto its side.

As they'd been doing all morning, two of the crew members stretched out the animal by the front and back legs and held it still while the other quickly seared a "WP" on its right upper hip. He returned the branding iron to the fire and they released the calf. Jumping to its feet, it hopped and bucked away from the men before it turned to bleat its displeasure.

Clint, who'd reined his horse to a stop next to Mike, chuckled. "Feisty little devil." To the others, he said, "That's the last one. Let's grab our stuff and call it a morning." He coiled the rope, dropped it around his saddlehorn and climbed off his horse.

117

One of the men lifted the branding iron from the fire and threw it into a snowbank, where it sizzled and steamed. Another shoveled snow onto the flames.

Clint helped Mike disconnect the fence panels. "If I do say so myself, these worked great."

"Your modification to the plans we found on the Internet was just what we needed." They laid a panel on the ground. "Don't know if you heard," Mike said. "That was my mom on the radio."

Clint shook his head.

"She's on her way to Dymple's house. Left chili in the slow cooker. Want to help me eat it?"

"You don't have to ask twice." Clint grinned. "Besides the fact it's slim pickin's in my cupboards, your mom makes the best chili in the West."

"I won't argue with that. Come over to the house after you drop off the equipment. I'll take care of the horses."

Clint helped the men carry panels to the flatbed trailer attached to his pickup, while Mike loaded the horses, tack and all, into the horse trailer behind his truck. He was getting inside when the first snowflake landed on his sleeve. He studied the darkening sky. The soil needed the moisture, but as far as he was concerned, they'd had enough winter. He was ready for spring.

He started the engine and pulled out in front of the others. They hadn't traveled far when he rounded a bend and came upon an old Ford pickup parked crosswise on the dirt road, high-centered in a snowdrift.

Cyrus. What's he doing down here? Mike rolled down his window.

The wizened, cussing man was outside his pickup, shoveling snow mixed with dirt in front of a back wheel.

Mike stopped his truck and got out, Tramp right behind him. "What's goin' on, Cyrus?" Exhaust fumes and a burnt rubber smell tinged the cooling air.

Without glancing up, Cyrus said, "You got eyes. You can see for yourself."

Mike ignored the growl in his gravelly voice. "We'll push you out."

Cyrus scowled. "I'm takin' off." He climbed into his truck and revved the engine. But when the wheels spun without catching, he got out again.

One of the horses in the trailer whinnied and the wind picked up. Snowflakes swirled around them.

"I've got a bucket of sand in the back." Mike flipped his coat collar up around his neck. "I can throw down—"

"I don't need your two cents." Cyrus glared at him. "Just 'cause your dad ain't around any longer and you got those high-falutin' university degrees doesn't mean you can tell me what to do."

Mike stared back. What got stuck in your craw, old man? Cyrus was one of those who thought higher education was a waste of time. He'd even heard him say it rotted the brain. But what did that have to do with pushing him out of a snowdrift?

Clint and the others walked up. "Hey, Cyrus, good timing," Clint said. "A little muscle power from these guys and we'll have you out of there faster 'n you can say giddy-up."

Cyrus glowered at Clint and then at the men who were taking positions behind his truck's tailgate. "I don't need no—"

Mike and Clint joined the others.

Without another word, Cyrus hopped into his pickup. The moment he put it in gear, the men began to push. Dirt-darkened snow sprayed from the spinning wheels, coating their jeans. But within seconds, the Ford was out of the snowdrift and charging up the road, rattling all the way.

Swiping at his pantlegs, Clint walked over to Mike, who was doing the same. "So he didn't think he needed help, huh?"

"He's in one of his moods."

Clint grunted. "He better not grouse at the guests."

"I'll say something if he gets to bellyaching around the dining hall." His dad had been able to talk sense into Cyrus when he got testy. Now Mike wished he knew what he said to him. He rubbed his gloves together to knock off the dirty snow. With any luck, the crotchety old guy would simmer down and behave himself during their guest season.

He was sliding behind the wheel again, when he saw taillights at the top of the hill in the distance. Cyrus's pickup backed over the ridge and rolled slowly toward them, stopping just the other side of the snowdrift. Mike rolled up his window and stepped out of his vehicle.

After he told Tramp to "stay," he closed the door to block the snow that was blowing in. Clint joined him. Trudging through the dirt-darkened slush, the two approached the Ford truck's passenger side.

Clint muttered, "Maybe he's gonna apologize."

"That's as likely as me running for mayor next year."

"I'll vote for you. Twice."

"I won't visit you in jail, but Cyrus might."

Clint was still chuckling when they got to the pickup.

Cyrus got out and faced them. "The only reason I was down in these parts was because some yahoo left the gate open and that mare your mom's been working with took off." He gripped the side of the truck bed. "I turned around when I saw you were branding. Figured if she'd come this far, you'd have seen her. That's when my rig got stuck."

Mike frowned. His dad's horse had been penned with the mare. "Everyone around here knows not to—"

"You talking about the horse that got wrapped in barbed wire?" Clint asked.

"Yeah. Flighty as a feral cat and just as hard to catch."

The mare, which belonged to a neighbor, had been traumatized by the experience as well as injured, mostly due to panic and flailing legs. The vet had prescribed antibiotics, but a couple ugly wounds still leaked fluid and radiated heat, and the horse had little interest in eating.

"I figured it out," Cyrus said, "when I saw your dad's gelding wandering over by the dining hall like a lost kid. He's back in the corral."

Mike nodded. "Thanks." His mom had put the two horses together to keep each other company. She would have been a wreck if Dad's horse had disappeared, not to mention the neighbor's mare.

Cyrus brushed snow from his jacket sleeves. "If it keeps snowing like this, I won't be able to see a gol durn thing from the road. But I'll keep lookin'."

Wet snow pummeled Mike's face. He tipped his hat brim low and turned to Clint. "You game to ride into the trees? The mare might be headed through the hills to get to her home ranch."

"Sure thing. I'll ask one of the guys to drive my truck so they can unload the corral panels when they get back. What's the horse's name?"

"Uh..." Mike gave him a sheepish half-grin." Twinkle Hooves."

Clint's eyebrows rose. "Twinkle Hooves?"

"Belongs to a teenage girl."

"Say no more." Clint held up his gloved palm. "My niece over in Lander named her guinea pig 'Muffin Sunshine Whisper.'" He grimaced. "Go figure." Pulling his hat low, he added, "For the record, no way am I going to ride through the trees yelling, 'Oh, Twinkle Hooves...' He placed his hand next to his mouth. "Where are you?'"

"Mom calls the mare 'Twink.'"

"That's more like it."

"I'm gonna take off," Cyrus said. "See what I can see." He reached into the truck bed and grabbed a halter and lead rope. "You'll need these."

Mike leaned across to take them from him. "Thanks."

With that, Cyrus climbed into his truck and drove away.

Clint watched him go. "Did he just flip a switch in his brain or what? That was like night and day."

"He's done it before. This time, the switch probably has more to do with his love for horses than anything."

The Ford topped the hill and disappeared.

Mike turned to Clint. "I hate to waste manpower hunting for a horse in the middle of a snowstorm when we have plenty else to do. But we're responsible for that mare." He motioned to where the other men waited in a pickup. "Have the guys drive around the backside of the ranch. It's not likely she's gone that direction or that far, but we'd better cover all bases."

The two returned to their trucks to strap on handguns and don slickers. Mike unloaded the horses while Clint gave the men instructions and Tramp sniffed the rocks and sagebrush bushes on each side of the road. Mike debated the wisdom of taking the dog with them. The going could get rough, what with wet ground, rocky terrain and the snow that was now coming down fast and furious. But Tramp would be an asset in tracking the horse. He had a good nose on him.

When he asked his foreman his opinion, Clint gave him an immediate thumbs-up. "I say take him. Tramp's a sharp dog."

They mounted their horses and started up the hill, Tramp trailing behind. Although the snow from the previous storm had mostly melted beneath the dried grass and sagebrush, new snow was already blanketing the landscape. Mike tried to lead them around, not through the drifts. But when they got higher on the mountain, either snow or rocks or both blocked their path.

He circumvented a massive stack of boulders and worked into the trees. The snow silenced all sound except for an occasional horse snuffle and the wind that whistled clean and crisp through the aspen grove's barren, white-trunked trees. Deeper in the forest, snow-trimmed evergreens—spruces, firs and pines—replaced the aspen and cut the wind.

At the higher elevation, where the sun rarely broke through, snow still blanketed the ground. He came across a trampled deer trail. Pleased to find a route through the woods, Mike turned in time to see Tramp hop a snow-covered log and flounder in a hole on the other side. "Whoa!" Mike reined to a stop, dropped the reins and trudged through the frozen branches and rocks that littered the snowy forest floor to help his dog. But Tramp scrambled out of the hole before he reached him.

"Better follow me, buddy." He patted the dog's head. "No sniffing around."

Tramp shook snow from his coat.

"Mike…" Cyrus's raspy, muffled voice emanated from within his slicker. "You hear me?"

Mike reached beneath the yellow raincoat for the radio on his belt. "Yeah, Cyrus, I hear you."

"Hard to tell with the snow coming down so hard, but I'm fairly certain I see horse tracks headed up the hill. I'm a couple miles from the ranch, so if you're aimed this direction, there's a chance you'll run into the mare."

"I appreciate the update."

Clint broke into the conversation. "That's good news. We're on the right track."

"Buzz me if you need anything," Cyrus said. "I'll be working in the dining hall, getting it ready for next week."

"Clint, where are you?" Mike asked.

"I thought I saw something move," came the crackling reply, "so I waited and watched, but then it was gone. Coulda been the horse or another animal—or just my imagination." He paused. "I'm wondering how we're going to see a white horse on a day like today."

"If she's in the trees, she won't be as hard to spot."

"Good thought. Be there in a minute."

Mike did a three-sixty, examining the spaces between every boulder, bush and tree in sight. But he didn't see any horses, white or otherwise. He knew Lightning would call out a greeting the moment he caught wind of the mare. Yet, he continued his search.

A crow cawed from somewhere above him. Mike craned his neck. A solitary black bird perched high in a ponderosa pine stared down at him through the curtain of snow. Its head was cocked as if it wondered what kind of creatures would venture into the forest on such a day.

When Clint came around the bend, Mike nudged Lightning. They moved slowly along the trail. Scanning their surroundings, he watched for movement and listened for noises other than the crunch of their horses' hooves in the snow. A wind gust whooshed through the trees and snow showered from a big branch ahead.

Tramp growled.

Mike turned in the saddle. "What is it?"

His dog had stopped in the middle of the trail. Legs stiff, tail straight, he peered into the trees, nostrils twitching. After a long moment, he relaxed.

Clint rode up behind Mike.

"Any idea what Tramp saw?" Mike asked.

"Nope." Clint shook his head. "But I don't doubt for a moment that he caught wind of something. Maybe it was whatever I saw earlier."

A clump of snow fell onto Mike's hat. He glanced at the snow-laden tree branch above him and moved out from under it. "One thing for sure, it wasn't the runaway. Tramp wouldn't growl at a horse." He shook the snow off the hat and brushed his shoulders.

"Could be a hungry critter. If it is, I hope it doesn't run across the mare."

"Yeah, I was thinking the same thing." A sick, domesticated horse would be easy prey, especially a horse with oozing wounds a predator's sensitive nostrils could easily detect. Mike put on his hat and urged his horse forward, running through a mental list of wild animals in the area.

Wolves were rare in their part of the country, but that didn't mean one hadn't wandered into the Sierra Madres. Bears were more common. A neighbor had recently spotted a female with two cubs, which meant most, if not all, bears had come out of hibernation. And mountain lions were always a threat. He'd heard one scream just last night. Bobcats sometimes attacked sheep, but he doubted one would take on a horse.

He studied their snow-muffled environment. Knowing that something might be following them gave him an eerie feeling. He patted the handgun strapped to his side beneath the slicker, grateful they'd come prepared for trouble.

Squirrel chatter fractured the stillness and Tramp bounded forward, barking. A gray squirrel sat on a low tree branch, tugging pine nuts from a pinecone with its teeth and dropping the brown scales on the snow-covered ground below. The noisy rodent scolded the intruders between nibbles.

Tramp sat at the base of the tree, wagging his tail and yapping at the squirrel.

As he passed the dog, Mike called to him, "Come on, Tramp."

The big dog took off, plunging through a drifted area and around a bend in the trail.

"Your dog's having a great time," Clint said. A moment later, he added, "Now that we're out of the wind, I have to agree. It's good to be in the mountains after a long winter."

"Yeah. I just hope that mare didn't go far."

Before they'd finished navigating the curve around the mountain, Tramp came running back, snow puffs swirling behind him.

"Hey, boy," Mike said.

The dog whined twice then turned around, starting back the way he came.

"You see something?"

Tramp whined again.

Mike snapped the reins. His horse broke into a trot and they followed the dog. Just beyond the next crook in the trail, Lightning neighed and a response came from an aspen grove farther along the path. Mike reined to a halt and stared between snowflakes until, finally, he spotted the mare.

Standing beside the deer trail amidst white aspen trunks and backed by snow-covered rocks, the mare blended with the surroundings like a Bev Doolittle painting.

Tramp's gaze flicked from the mare to him and then to the mare again.

Clint came alongside him. His horse nickered, and Clint glanced at Mike. "You see her?"

"You were right." Mike indicated the aspen grove. "She's hard to spot."

"Oh, yeah, there she is." Clint laughed. "It's a case of not seeing the horse for the forest rather than not seeing the forest for the trees."

The mare eyed them, ears flicked forward. Her tail switched and she pawed the ground, as if readying to run at the slightest hint of danger.

"You think you can get a rope through those trees if we move closer?" Mike asked. Clint was the best roper in the state. However, an airborne loop might catch on branches.

Before Clint could respond, Tramp scampered to the mare.

Mike didn't call him back. "That might be our answer right there," he said. "Those two get along good."

The dog and the horse touched noses.

"Bring her here, Tramp," Mike called. "Bring Twink to us."

Tramp ran their way, but the horse didn't follow. The dog glanced back as if to say, "Come on." Then without warning, he spun around, growling, and charged toward the horse as a coyote appeared behind the mare—and another and another.

More snapping, yipping coyotes, their hackles bristling, sprang from the bushes to pounce on Tramp. The dog yelped and was immediately embroiled in a snarling, howling mass of gray and yellow fur.

The mare pivoted and galloped up the trail away from the men, her white mane flying and two coyotes nipping at her hind legs. Her pounding hooves churned snow chunks into the air.

Mike and Clint drew their guns from beneath their slickers, aimed upward and fired. Snow plopped off the tree branches as they charged the coyotes. The pack broke apart, but Tramp tore into the nearest coyote, a big one. They circled, fangs bared, growling. Mike would have shot the coyote, but he couldn't chance hitting his dog.

Barking and yipping, other coyotes moved to rejoin the battle. Before they could attack Tramp, Mike and Clint fired and fired again. Three animals stumbled and fell. The others whimpered, turned tail and disappeared behind the boulders.

The horses snorted and pranced.

Gun ready, Mike jumped off Lightning and ran toward Tramp and the remaining coyote, yelling and waving his hat. "Git out of here, git!"

The feral creature took one look at him, snarled and slunk into the trees.

Mike shouted to Clint, "Cover me!" He knelt to check Tramp's injuries. "Come here, boy."

Still alert to danger, the dog didn't seem to know he was there. Deep, guttural threats rumbling in his throat, he smelled the prostrate animals from one end to the other before sniffing the blood splatters and gray fur clumps scattered about the trampled snow. Lifting his head, he eyed the woods, ears pricked and nostrils quivering.

Mike stood. The smell of blood and beast shrouded the narrow clearing, but from what he could tell, his dog was okay. He was bloody, but he was moving. "Come on, Tramp. Let's go find Twink."

The dog darted to a tree trunk. He put his nose to it, sniffed, and then scurried to a second tree and a third.

"Tramp!"

The dog glanced at him.

"Now! Find Twink." He tromped through the snow to where Clint was holding the reins of both skittish horses in one hand and his gun in the other, scanning all directions.

Mike mounted his wild-eyed horse. Lightning's ears stood upright above his rigid neck. "Take off," Mike yelled, pointing the direction the mare had bolted. "He'll follow."

Clint wheeled his horse around. Mike did the same. As they thundered up the snowy deer path, he glanced back in time to see Tramp leap onto the trail.

They heard the mare—and the coyotes—before they saw them.

The horse hadn't gotten far. Surrounded by the yipping, howling pack, the mare was backed against a rock outcropping. Blood dripped down her haunches. Ears flat against her head, she squealed and reared on her hind legs, striking out with her forelegs. One hoof caught a coyote in the chest and sent it flying across the clearing into a tree trunk. It yelped and plunged to the ground.

Yelling and firing shots overhead, Mike and Clint rushed the coyotes. The frenzied animals twisted away from the horse, and the men shot into the pack. One fell. The others fled into the frozen forest, scattering as they ran.

Tramp caught up and started after the coyotes, but Mike shouted for him to stay. The dog obeyed but continued to bark and growl. He smelled the fallen animals, and apparently convinced they were no longer a threat, went to the mare. Again, the two touched noses.

Clint blew out a long breath. "Feels like one of those nights when you have the same nightmare over and over. Coyotes don't usually attack horses."

"They may have sensed the mare's weakness or smelled her wounds." Mike indicated the coyotes on the ground. "Or, by the looks of them, they were just plain hungry. It's been a long winter."

"Yeah, that's the scrawniest pack of coyotes I've ever seen."

"I think we've left them enough fresh meat that they'll leave us alone. Some people say coyotes don't eat their own, but I disagree. If they're hungry enough, they'll eat anything. They're probably already gnawing on the carcasses back where they first attacked the mare."

Mike pulled the halter and lead rope off the saddle horn and dismounted. "But just in case they decide to go after the mare again, you might stand guard while I try to catch her."

He clipped the lead rope to the halter and walked slowly toward the horse and dog, all the while murmuring, "Keep her there, Tramp. Keep her there." He stopped several feet from the pair. "It's all right, Twink. Everything's gonna be fine, girl. Just fine."

She flipped one of her ears toward him, but her neck remained high and taut. He knew she was listening for coyotes with her other ear, and he didn't blame her for staying alert. But he had to convince her the danger had passed. "Just stay where you are, Twink." He kept his voice soft. "And we'll lead you to a nice, warm barn and a bucket full of grain."

Clint brought the other horses closer.

Lightning nickered and the mare answered. She lowered her head a couple inches and relaxed her ears and tail.

Mike took another step.

"Hey," Clint said, his voice low, "I just remembered I have a bag of little carrots in my coat pocket. I stuck it in there the yesterday and forgot all about it."

"Carrots?" Mike looked at him. "Since when do you snack on vegetables?"

"Since my health-conscious sister visited last week and left two bags in my fridge. I think she was trying to give me a hint." He undid his slicker, reached inside and leaned over to hand Mike the sack.

"I'll offer her one," Mike said. "However, Mom says Twink is off her feed, so she may not respond."

Although both Clint's horse and Mike's nickered their interest, Mike held the carrots out for the mare to see. Her nostrils flared. He took another step. The horse eyed the carrots.

He pulled off his gloves, opened the sack and offered her one small carrot, which she took without hesitation. "Good girl," he whispered. After giving her another, he unzipped one of the slicker's deep pockets, dropped the carrots in and held out the halter.

She sniffed the worn leather briefly before shoving her nose into the pocket. Mike laughed. "First things first, huh?"

Clint chuckled. "And they say the way to a man's heart is through his stomach. The Twink just proved females are no different."

Mike draped the lead rope over the mare's neck, grabbing the loose end so she'd know she wasn't going anywhere on her own again. And then he slipped the halter over her nose and buckled it behind her ears. She shook her head, but she didn't try to escape.

He rewarded her with a handful of carrots and before they took off, he treated the other horses to the remaining carrots in the bag.

"These two did okay." Clint patted his horse's neck. "They coulda panicked and run off, and that pack of coyotes would have had a heyday."

"Yeah, and you and I would have had a long, cold hike home."

Winds of Hope

Mike and Clint parted ways at the crest of the hill. Clint turned to head back the way they'd come. He would return to Mike's truck and drive it to the ranch headquarters, while Mike led The Twink, as Clint called her, homeward through the steadily falling snow.

The horse followed quietly behind Lightning, head down, tail limp. Mike hoped that meant she was glad to have someone else in charge of her safety, not that she was ill. She had new wounds and she was obviously tired, but she didn't limp. They weren't far from the barn—just one more snow-covered hill to climb.

To his relief, they made it home without incident. He dismounted to open the barn door and lead the horses inside. Tramp darted ahead but stopped in the middle of the barn to give his thick, bloodied coat a good shake.

When Mike untied Twink's lead line from the saddle horn, Lightning nickered and headed straight for his stall. Mike led the mare into an adjoining stall, where she glanced at her surroundings and then stood stock-still. Her head drooped, along with her ears and eyelids.

He took off his slicker and hung it on a nail. Either the horse was too spent to react or she'd accepted the fact he wanted to help her, not harm her. He hoped it was the latter. She'd endured more than enough trauma. He shook snow from his hat and hooked it over the slicker.

Tramp curled on a clump of straw in the corner and went to sleep. Mike eyed him for a moment. His dog seemed okay, but he'd ask Doc Hall to come as soon as possible to check both Tramp and the horse.

The familiar aromas of damp dog, wet horse and tangy, earthy hay filled the stall. Talking softly to the mare, Mike removed the halter and wiped moisture off her body, careful not to press against the scars or the new wounds that blazed through her coat. Her skin twitched a couple times, but she didn't pull away.

Normally, he would have finished off with a curry comb and brush and a hoof pick to remove ice and mud from her hooves. However, the horse had resisted grooming since she'd tangled with the barbed wire. He cleansed her wounds, secured their warmest horse blanket around her torso and filled the grain and water buckets. Doc Hall could decide if she needed further treatment.

The mare nosed at the feed. "That a girl," he murmured. "Eat up." Exiting the stall, he latched the gate behind him and went to the phone that hung on the wall by the door. His mom would be anxious to assess the horse's condition.

When she didn't answer, he remembered her lunch with Dymple and hoped she hadn't attempted to drive home in the storm. She could check the mare later and let the owner know they were calling the vet to examine the horse. But as far as he could tell, The Twink had weathered her afternoon adventure in decent shape, considering what she'd been through.

From the shelf above the sink in the corner, he grabbed the jar of Bag Balm. Although the concoction was meant for cow udders, area ranchers had used the stuff for years to relieve dry hands and bleeding, split skin on their knuckles. Wyoming's arid climate was hard on a body. And then he'd read an article about the cadaver-sniffing dogs tasked with searching the World Trade Center rubble. Their handlers had soothed the dogs' sore paws with Bag Balm. That's when he began using it on Tramp's paws, especially on days like today when he'd spent hours running in the snow.

Returning to The Twink's stall, he called his dog. Tramp lifted his head but didn't move. Mike held out the jar. Tramp got to his feet, slipped through the rails and plopped down on his side. Mike chuckled. His dog loved to have his paws massaged. After cleaning and drying each paw, he applied the Bag Balm. Tramp let out a long sigh and promptly fell asleep.

That task completed, Mike removed the saddle, saddle blanket and pad from Lightning's back and wiped down the stallion. After a quick workover with the curry comb and brush, he picked the horse's hooves, placed a horse blanket across his back, and watered and fed him. The activity got his blood flowing again, warming him to his fingertips.

With both horses dry and contentedly munching, he climbed the ladder to the hayloft. Mike chuckled. Maybe the mare just needed a good run—and a chance to kick a coyote or two.

For a moment, he stood between haybales, remembering how he'd loved the creaky loft and the smell of hay and horses ever since he was a kid. He and his brother, Matt, had spent many an hour daydreaming together there and playing ranch with a plastic barn and miniature cows and horses.

He was shoving a hay bale toward the edge of the loft to drop to the floor below, when Tramp snarled long and low. What now? Mike waited, listening. Could the day go any more haywire than it already had? If a skunk had snuck inside to escape the storm…

His dog growled again, this time louder. Mike leaned on the bale and peered over the side. A man wearing a cowboy hat stood below him. Elbows bent and fists clenched, he was apparently in a showdown with Tramp. The dog crouched in front of the man, legs planted and hackles high.

Mike frowned. "Hello?"

The man, a neighbor, glared up at Mike. "Call off your dog."

"Hughes." Mike dug his fingers into the dry, scratchy hay. Should have known. Tramp had always been a good judge of character. "What brings you over here in the middle of a storm?"

His dad had told him Todd Hughes had an unnerving way of appearing without a sound. If Tramp hadn't warned him, he wouldn't have known he was in their barn. He climbed down the ladder and walked over to the rigid, rumbling dog.

"It's okay, boy." Placing his hand on the dog's warm head, he felt the reverberations emanating from his throat. "Good job. I'll take it from here. Sit."

The dog sat but remained on-guard, ears forward, eyes on Todd.

"What can I do for you?" Mike straightened.

Todd scanned the barn's interior, as if assessing its value. "Nice barn."

Mike waited. Hughes hadn't driven over in a snowstorm to admire their barn.

Finally, Todd met his gaze. "I'm here to find out what I can do for you."

"Oh, yeah?" Mike couldn't hide his doubt. Todd Hughes was not known for his helpfulness. In fact, the opposite was true. But how to deal with the arrogant man? This was one of the many times he missed his dad. He would have known what to say, what to do.

"With Dan gone and summer coming, you're in way over your head with this guest ranch of yours. If you want to stay in operation, you're gonna need some help. I'm here to lend a hand."

"Mom and I have plenty of help."

"Your mother is in mourning and, well..." He shrugged. "She's a woman. She's weak. She won't be—"

"Enough." Mike raised his palm.

"Go ahead, stick your head in a haystack." Todd jutted his chin. "But don't forget, I've got the experience, the know-how, and the wisdom you need." He looked Mike up and down. "Took you long enough to graduate college."

Mike didn't bother with a response. Six years for an undergraduate degree plus a master's degree was right on schedule in his book. He thought of Cyrus. Why were people he'd known for years all of a sudden hassling him about his education?

Todd leaned his head back. "Yeah, took a real long time." He stared at the rafters. "Costs a lot to keep a place like this going. I can float you a loan, give you the neighbor rate."

Mike squinted at him. Strange way to offer help. "I've got work to do." He folded his arms." You know where the door is."

"Ha." Todd's eyes flashed. "Guess you don't know how to take friendly, neighborly advice."

Tramp growled and Todd began to back toward the door. "Don't say I didn't warn you."

❧

Mike checked his watch. Ten after four. "Well, Clint, this is more like supper than lunch, but the chili's still plenty hot." He bit into a piece of warm cornbread dripping with butter.

"Definitely worth the wait." Clint sprinkled grated cheese on his chili. "Knowing we'd eventually return to your mom's cornbread and chili kept me going this afternoon." He leaned over the steaming bowl and inhaled. "Mm-mm. The smell alone could hold me for hours." He took a bite and brandished his spoon. "Yep, as good as ever."

Mike nodded. He didn't want his mom to take care of him, but he had to admit coming home to a hot bowl of chili wasn't so bad. His chili never turned out as good.

"Sure glad we found the mare before the coyotes did her in."

"Yeah," Mike said. "It was all about teamwork today. Cyrus saw the tracks and Tramp alerted us to the horse—and the coyotes."

"Tramp was a big help cutting the calves from the herd this morning and fearless when those coyotes attacked him and The Twink."

Tramp, sprawled on a rug in front of the fire, elevated his head at the mention of his name.

"Good job, boy." Mike said. "You did okay today." He smiled at Clint. "I'm proud of him." His collie had been a gutsy go-getter ever since he was a puppy, but this was the first time he'd taken on a pack of coyotes.

Tramp blew out a breath and dropped his head back down on the rug.

"And The Twink," Clint said. "She must have knocked that coyote twenty feet before it slammed into the tree."

Mike laughed. "That was like a scene from a movie. Don't think I'll ever forget it."

"She was sleeping when I unloaded my horse in the barn," Clint said. "But she seemed okay, from what I could see."

"She's probably more exhausted than anything. Doc Hall will be here first thing in the morning to check out her and Tramp."

They got down to the business of eating. Three-and-a-half bowls later, Mike asked, "How long before we brand that last bunch of calves?"

"Two weeks, three at the most. That way, some of the guests will get to watch."

Mike wondered what his mom would think about the delay, but he said, "Glad you're staying on top of the working side of the ranch. Mom and I are scrambling to pull things together on the guest side. As you know, I didn't have much to do with guests in the past."

"Gotta be tough for both of you, but you'll do okay." Clint paused. "I sure miss your dad. He was a good man and a great boss. How long has it been since the cancer took him? Five, six months?"

"Just over seven months now."

Clint sighed. "That long already... Hard to believe. Seems like his funeral was just a couple weeks ago. How's your mom doing?"

"She puts on a smile every day, but I can tell she's lonely. Not that I don't miss Dad—believe me, I feel his absence, but my parents had a special kind of marriage. They were close."

"I could see that. Made me reconsider bachelorhood now and then."

Mike pulled back the foil and cut two more pieces of cornbread from the pan. "Yeah, I know what you mean." Like Clint, he wasn't in a rush to get married, but if he ever did, he'd want a union like his folks had.

Although he didn't see a need for a wife right now, he had to admit he had his lonely moments. He missed the gang he'd hung out with at UW. And he missed the fun he'd had dating, despite the fact he'd never gotten serious with any of the girls.

Lately, he'd been missing his talks with his dad. On cold nights, they'd sit in front of the fire with mugs of hot cider. In the summer, they'd relax on the back deck, cold beers in hand, talking over the day's events. A girlfriend or a wife to talk with might be okay, but no one could replace Dad.

He'd learned so much from his father, yet he didn't feel equipped to step into his boots. Todd Hughes's slurs had cut closer to the bone that he'd ever admit to anyone but himself. How much help would he be to his mom this summer while she was trying to keep on top of the guest season without Dad at the helm?

"Oh, yeah...Mom." Mike jumped up and strode across the room to the living area. The wood floor groaned with every step of his boots. He picked up the phone by the couch and saw the message light was blinking. Sure enough, she'd left a voice mail saying the storm was supposed to end around four, followed by sunshine that would melt the snow on the highway. "And, good news," she said, "a chinook wind is coming our way this evening."

He walked to a window to pull back a curtain. "The snow stopped. Mom says a chinook is s'posed to blow through later."

"Good," Clint said, "That'll help dry this place before the guests arrive."

Mike had barely sat down when the phone rang. He got to his feet again and grabbed the receiver. "Hello."

A feminine voice purred, "Hello, Mikey. How you doing? We haven't seen each other in a while. I was thinking we should find a cozy—"

"Can't talk right now. I have company."

"Maybe later we can—"

"Goodbye." He replaced the phone, sat down and took a bite of chili.

"I'm not company." Clint buttered another piece of cornbread. "You coulda talked to that person."

Mike snorted. "Tara Hughes?"

"Uh-oh." Clint's brow crumpled. "She's hounded you for years."

"You'd think she would have gotten the message by now."

"Have you ever flat out told her to hightail it out of your life?"

144

"Yeah, tried that once." Mike grunted. "She fell all over me, sobbing like a kid being dragged out of a toy store. Thought I'd never escape her tentacles." He ran his fingers through his hair. "I've been tempted to deck the woman a time or two, But that's the problem—she's a woman."

Clint laughed. "I'm pretty sure you could get by with it, if you do it around here, where the deputies are well aware of her daddy's-girl tactics."

"Reminds me—that daddy of hers snuck into our barn today."

"Todd Hughes?" Clint sat back. "When was that?"

"Right after I returned with the horses. I didn't hear him come in, but Tramp had a fit."

"Tramp's a smart dog."

The dog lifted his head again.

Clint gave him a thumbs-up. "Way to go, Tramp." He turned to Mike. "What did he want?"

"He said he has the wisdom and experience to help me run the ranch, now that Dad's gone."

Clint arched an eyebrow. "Did you tell him to go jump in a snowbank?"

"I told him to leave…after he insulted Mom and offered to loan me money so we don't go belly up."

"Todd and Tara Hughes…" Clint shook his head. "Talk about a couple nutty neighbors you could do without."

"Yeah." Mike blew out a long breath. "I'd like to think this is the last we hear from them, but..." He rubbed his jaw. "What a day this has been. I sure hope it's not an indication of what the upcoming guest season holds for us."

Want to Read More?

I hope you enjoyed *Winds of Hope* and that you'll consider leaving a review or rating on Amazon, Barnes & Noble, Goodreads, or wherever you like to share your thoughts about books. If you'd like to learn about future releases, I invite you to visit my website – beckylyles.com – to register for my (rare and random) newsletter. You'll receive a free eBook short-story collection titled *Passageways* as my "thank you."

– Other Novels in the Kate Neilson Series –

WINDS OF WYOMING (Book One in the Kate Neilson Series)

Fresh out of a Pennsylvania penitentiary armed with a marketing degree, Kate Neilson heads to Wyoming anticipating an anonymous new beginning as a guest-ranch employee. A typical twenty-five-year-old woman might be looking to lasso a cowboy, but her only desire is to get on with life on the outside—despite her growing interest in the ranch owner. When she discovers a violent ex-lover followed her west, she fears the past she hoped to hide will trail as close as a shadow and imprison her once again.

"Though Rebecca Carey Lyles knows how to mix suspense with the perfect amounts of warmth and humor, I found that the flaws in her characters were really what drew me in. *Winds of Wyoming* is the kind of book that gets readers hooked and asking for more."

Angela Ruth Strong, author of *Lighten Up, The Fun4Hire Series, False Security, Finding Love in Sun Valley, Idaho,* and *Finding Love in Big Sky, Montana*

WINDS OF FREEDOM (Book Two in the Kate Neilson Series)

Winter storms blast across the West and fuel the bitter wind that ravages ranch-owner Kate Neilson Duncan's soul. In the midst of shattered dreams, she learns her best friend has not only disappeared, she's been accused of murder. Kate vows to find her and prove her innocence. When the Duncans' Wyoming ranch is threatened and Kate's mother-in-law becomes ensnared by evil, Kate and her husband, Mike, join forces with their foreman to fight for all that is dear to them. Can the three ranchers defeat the lethal powers determined to destroy Kate, their loves ones and their ranch?

"*Winds of Freedom* by Rebecca Lyles is not only an entertaining read, it is another courageous assault on the hideous crime of human trafficking. I applaud the author's willingness to tackle this topic and to help educate us in the depth of its evil. Awareness is the first step in setting the captives free—and then the challenge to each of us to get involved. Together we can make a difference! Do not miss this excellent book!"

Kathi Macias, award winning author of more than 50 books, including the *Freedom Series,"* novels written around the topic of human trafficking

WINDS OF CHANGE (Book Three in the Kate Neilson Series)

Kate Neilson Duncan discovers new purpose for her life when she and her mother-in-law, Laura Duncan, open a home on their Wyoming guest ranch for young trafficking victims. But her husband, Mike Duncan, insists the endless hours Kate spends at the children's home threaten their marriage. Following an argument with Mike, Kate treats three of the kids to an outing—where the unimaginable happens. If Kate and the children survive, can she and Mike recover what they've lost?

Powerful Conclusion to the Kate Neilson Series. Intense page-turner. Opened my eyes to the cruelty and terror of human trafficking that is going on around us and throughout the world today. Showed the power of love, faith and hope to survive and overcome the worst of circumstances. Very well written. Steve Bower

– Other Books by the Author –

Short Stories —

PASSAGEWAYS: A Short Story Collection

Four authors who also happen to be friends. Sixteen unique short stories. From tales of spies and trains and John Wayne, to monks, magic and marriage, readers will be entertained, challenged and inspired. Valerie D. Gray, Lisa Michelle Hess, Peter Leavell and Rebecca Carey Lyles met several years ago at a newly formed writers group in a back corner of Rediscovered Books, an Idaho indie bookstore. Over time, they became critique partners who share the ups and downs of the writing life as well as act as first readers for one another's work.

Great stories, very eclectic variety, which was uber enjoyable for me! Each story was like opening a surprise gift. Sandra Doerty

While the authors, their styles and their stories are very diverse, Passageways is a uniformly excellent read. Entertaining to the very last page! Pat W.

Nonfiction —

IT'S A GOD THING! Inspiring Stories of Life-Changing Friendships"

When it seemed the best years of his life were over, Larry Baker gained a new passion for living through unexpected, life-changing friendships and adventures. He invites you to join him in the daily exhilaration of discovering the surprises and relationships God has waiting for each of us, just around the corner.

"It's a God Thing! is a very inspiring book that shows how God will use any willing heart in helping others come to the saving grace of Christ Jesus." Teresa Britton

ON A WING AND A PRAYER: Stories from Freedom Fellowship, a Prison Ministry

The night God told Donna Roth he was sending her to jail to share his love with incarcerated individuals, she said,

"Lord, you have the wrong house!" She had no experience or interest in prison ministry; yet, she was obedient, and Freedom Fellowship was formed. *"On a Wing and a Prayer"* features stories of inmates who found freedom inside prison walls through the ministry of Freedom Fellowship.

Acknowledgements

So many dear friends and family members took time from busy schedules to help me usher this book toward publication. Beta readers and proofreaders include Maureen Rose, Alissa Ketterling, Steve Lyles, Patricia Watkins, Valerie Gray, Lisa Hess, Jo Ann Gordon, Hilarey Johnson, Kathy Schuknecht, Michelle Netten, Corina Monoran, Pat Cory and Ruthann Batchelder. Horsewomen Patricia Watkins and Claudia Bernard graciously taught me about horse behavior, but please don't blame them if I got it wrong! Many thanks to each of you. Your insights and gentle corrections were just what I needed.

About the Author

Rebecca Carey Lyles grew up in Wyoming, the setting for her award-winning Kate Neilson novels. She currently lives in Idaho, where she serves as an editor and a mentor for aspiring authors. She and her husband, Steve, host a fun podcast they call "Let Me Tell You a Story." (beckylyles.com/podcast)

Contact the Author

Email: beckylyles@beckylyles.com

Facebook Author Page: Rebecca Carey Lyles

Blog: widgetwords.wordpress.com

Website: beckylyles.com

WINDS OF WYOMING

Book One in the Kate Neilson Series

Chapter One

Kate Neilson peered into the slot on the collection box lid. Was that money she saw on the bottom or crumpled paper? Sometimes people put weird stuff in offering boxes.

The early morning sunshine hadn't reached her side of the dark log chapel, but she didn't dare turn on the interior lights and attract attention. Maybe she should grab the flashlight from her car. Though she'd opened the side door at the front of the sanctuary, she still couldn't see inside the box.

She toyed with the padlock. All she needed was enough cash to get by until payday at her new job. If she left a note saying she'd pay it back right away, with interest, surely they'd understand. After all, she was down to her last ten—

The floor creaked.

Her heart stopped.

"That box is empty, sweetie."

Stifling a gasp, Kate dropped the lock and spun around.

A white-haired woman stood in the open doorway at the far end of the chapel.

"We haven't used it..." The woman's voice cracked. "Since two-thousand and three."

Kate darted for the foyer, her pulse pounding at her temple. No way were they going to catch her this time. She slammed against the front door. One twist of the handle and—

"Please don't leave."

Drawn by the plaintive plea, she glanced back.

"Didn't mean to scare you." The lady lifted the canvas bag she was carrying. "I came to arrange the flowers for this morning's service."

Kate hesitated, her heart drumming her ribs, her breath locked in her lungs.

The woman extended her palms. "Stay and visit. Please."

"I thought—" Kate released the breath and sucked in a gulp of dry mountain air. "I thought, because it's a church, it was okay to come inside. The door was unlocked. I..."

The lady's red-tinted lips parted in a wide, denture smile. "That's why we call this the Highway Haven House of God. We want travelers who've been enjoying the drive through the mountains to feel free to spend time with the creator of those hills." She hobbled toward the altar table at the front of the room. The wood floor squeaked with each step.

Kate clutched her chest to slow the hammering inside. What happened to the nerves of steel she'd honed on the streets of Pittsburgh? She took a breath. "I've never heard of a church called Highway Haven before."

The woman slid a vase from the center of the altar to the side. "Our little cathedral is a one-of-a-kind place, at least in Wyoming. Old-timers say this used to be the site of the rowdiest saloon this side of the Missouri, until..." She chuckled. "Until, as the story goes, a couple inebriated, arm-wrestling patrons knocked over a kerosene lamp, and the bar burped to the ground."

Burped? Kate squinted at her. How could someone with so many wrinkles, someone who said *burped* instead of *burned* call other people old-timers? Oh, well. At least she was harmless. Moving from the foyer into the sanctuary, Kate dropped into a pew at the back of the room.

The lady reached in her bag.

She's got a gun. Kate grabbed the bench in front of her, ready to dive beneath it.

But the smiling woman produced a tulip instead of a pistol. "My name is Miss Forbes. What's yours?" She pulled more tulips from her satchel.

Kate gripped the pew back. Wouldn't the cops love that? Her fingerprints *and* her name, even though she hadn't done anything wrong, this time.

After the tulips came lilac blossoms and a glass jar of water. Miss Forbes unscrewed the metal lid, poured the liquid into the vase, and added the flowers. She glanced at Kate, eyebrows raised.

Kate folded her arms and sat back.

"That's okay. I shouldn't be so nosey." Miss Forbes plucked a tulip from the arrangement. "For a long time, this

3

was just an ugly pile of blackened rubble. But in the early fifties, a small congregation purchased the land and built this chapel in two days." She indicated the walls, the flower in her fingers bobbing back and forth. "Raised the log walls the first day, added the roof the second."

She slipped the tulip into the center of the blossoms. "They called it Church on the Mountain."

Kate rubbed her stiff shoulder muscles and stared through the large window that dominated the front of the chapel. The opening framed a postcard-perfect scene of evergreens and newly leafed aspen in the foreground with snow-crowned peaks in the background—a far cry from the cement prison yard she'd circled twice a day for five long years.

If only she could immerse herself in her beautiful surroundings. But her mind wouldn't let go of the fact she hadn't heard the woman approach the building. She should have heard her footsteps outside the door, despite her slight stature.

She chewed at her bottom lip. A senile senior citizen had not only caught her off-guard but scared her half to death. Had she been seduced by the serenity of the place or too focused on the collection box?

Kate checked the windows again. No one else around. Standing, she stepped into the aisle and started for the front, determined to persuade the old lady to tell her where the church kept its stash. If she resisted, she'd explain her plan to repay the money. If that didn't work, she'd have to do a little arm twisting.

Her approach was no secret. The floor groaned with each footstep, but Miss Forbes continued to talk, her back to Kate. "Years later, after the state constructed a highway right next to the parking lot, the congregation decided it was time for a name change."

Six feet from the altar, Kate halted, knees flexed, feet planted wide.

The woman turned from the flowers, her hands on her waist. "Haven has a *peaceful* sound to it, don't you think?" Her blue eyes flashed. "Similar to *heaven*."

Kate flinched. *She knows. She knows what I was about to do.* She clenched her fists. *What's wrong with me? Why would I even consider harming an elderly person? Or helping myself to church money?* She wanted to run, but it was as though the woman's stare pinned her sandals to the floor.

Her shoulders sagged. Would she ever get it right? She could have stayed on her knees asking God to bless her new endeavor. That was the plan—to pray. She could have ignored the offering box. That would have been smart. She could have walked out the church door with God's favor and no regrets. That would have—

"Are you okay?"

At the sight of the woman's creased brow, Kate blinked and shifted her gaze. "I meant to stop at the overlook, but this little church seemed so inviting I stopped here first." The pungent perfume of the lilacs invaded her sinuses, making it hard to breathe.

Miss Forbes returned the vase to the center of the table, made some adjustments and smoothed the altar cloth. "The overlook is a half-mile down the road, well worth the stop. We also have a nice view from the rear of the church property. I can take you there, if you'd like. We have time before the church service begins."

Kate sneezed and rubbed her nose. "I would love to see it." She had to get out of the building before her sinuses swelled shut—and before she did something she'd regret the rest of her life, something that would put her back behind bars.

She followed Miss Forbes, who was shorter than she was by several inches, out the side door of the log structure and onto a dirt path that led into a shaded cemetery. Though the pink blossoms swinging at the end of her guide's long, white braid made her smile, all Kate could think about was how close she'd come to doing something really stupid again. Might as well bang on Patterson State Penitentiary's gate and beg the guards to let her back inside.

She'd left her past in Pittsburgh, but thieving was apparently as natural as breathing for her—no matter where she was or how fervently she promised God she would change her ways. No wonder cell doors were revolving doors for her. She shuddered. With the three-strikes-you're-out law, another mess-up would mean life without parole.

Shaking away the unbearable thought, she focused on the hillside cemetery speckled with headstones of every shape, tilt and shade of gray—and an occasional clump of snow. For the first time since they'd left the chapel, she heard the birds warble in the treetops and smelled the earthy, fresh fragrances of the forest—cleansing scents that soothed her spirit and cleared her head.

Miss Forbes paused to pluck a withered knot from a cluster of jonquils. Her braid slid forward to dangle above the flowers. "We had quite the storm a few days ago, full of moisture, which is fairly typical of spring snows around here. I didn't need to water the grass this morning, but I washed the grave markers." She straightened, her joints snapping. "Some think I'm silly, but my grandpa always said a society that honors the dead will honor the living."

She kicked a pinecone off the grass that topped a grave. "He was a deacon in this church for more than fifty yogurts." She pointed to tombstones several feet away. "His and Granny's stones are those two matching ones. My parents are buried next to them."

"*How long* was your grandpa a deacon?"

"For fifty…" Eyebrows scrunched, the woman turned to Kate. "Did I say something wrong?"

"I just didn't understand."

"It's not you, sweetie. It's me." The woman sighed. "My friends tell me I've been saying the craziest things ever since I tripped and hit my noggin on a headstone a couple years ago. They find it highly amusing. I'll be talking along fine then something silly pops out. The doctor says it's a form of ambrosia."

"You mean amnesia?"

The older lady pursed her wrinkled lips. "I don't know what I said, but my problem is called *aphasia*. I was told I might get over it—or I might not. The good news is that it's a language problem, not an intelligence issue, thank God." She snorted. "Although some might question that."

Kate knelt beside the markers. "You must have meant to say your grandpa was a deacon for fifty years."

"What did I say?"

"Uhm… Yogurts."

"Oh, my. No wonder my friends laugh."

"They shouldn't." Kate shook her head. "They must know what you're really thinking." She'd endured her share of ridicule in school and foster homes, not to mention prison.

Miss Forbes patted her shoulder. "Thank you, but they're just teasing. Sometimes I tease them, too."

Kate studied the gravestones. Damp granite glistened around the hand-etched engravings. *Otis Elmer Haggerty 1883-1966. Dymple Elizabeth Haggerty 1885-1973.* "Your grandparents were named Otis and Dymple?"

The lines at the woman's temples crinkled. "Yes, Granddad Otis and Granny Dymple."

"I never heard of anyone named Dymple before."

"Me neither, except for me."

"No kidding?"

"No kidding. I was born with a dimple in the middle of my chin, just like Granny. See?" She touched her chin.

Kate nodded, though she wasn't sure it was a dimple she saw or a crease. A single white hair jutted from a mole, brilliant in the morning sunlight.

"My parents used to say they argued about what to name me until the moment I was born. That's when they saw the dimple. I was named after both grandmothers. Dymple– with a *y*–Louise Forbes. You can call me Dymple."

Kate stood and offered her hand. "I'm Kate. Kate Neilson."

Dymple grasped her hand with both of hers, a look of recognition, maybe revelation flooding her face.

A chill shot up Kate's spine. She shouldn't have revealed her full name.

"Kate Neilson…" Dymple smiled. "I have a feeling you and I will become very good friends."

Winds of Wyoming

The trail wound through the cemetery and ended on a rock outcrop that overlooked a river. Bounded by a metal railing and topped with wrought-iron tables and chairs, the ledge looked as urbane as a backyard patio. Whiskey barrels scattered between the tables brimmed with pansies and petunias. Puffs of lobelia and tufts of sweet alyssum cascaded down the wooden sides.

Kate stepped to the railing. "This is a beautiful setting."

"Residents of our little community gather here often. We have parties, weddings, marshmallow roasts—all sorts of get-togethers on this rock patio."

"The flowers smell wonderful. I'm amazed the church has such beautiful flowers this high in the mountains—and this early in the summer."

"I trick them into early growth."

"Really?" Though the effervescent lady intrigued Kate, she wasn't ready to believe everything she said.

Dymple chuckled. "Really, but it's no trick. I have a little greenhouse in my garden, where I start my own plants early in the spring as well as seedlings for the church."

Kate leaned against the top railing. Below her, hummocks of snow clung to the rugged mountainside. Water seeped from the crusted mounds and trickled downhill to feed a river that ambled like a lazy snake through the verdant valley. She pointed to barely visible buildings at the far end of the basin. "Is that Copperville?"

"Sure is."

Rows of concrete cellblocks marched across Kate's memory. "Patterson is bigger than—"

"Bigger?"

Kate felt her cheeks warming and ducked her head. "The town is smaller than I expected."

"Copperville was a fair-sized mining town in the late eighteen-hundreds and early nineteen-hundreds." Dymple swept her hand across the panorama. "A hundred or so years later, as you can see, it isn't much more than a few businesses and a smattering of houses. I feel for those who couldn't make a living here, but I prefer a small community. Wouldn't live anywhere else."

"Too bad I left my camera in the car. My Great-Aunt Mary and my friend Amy in Pennsylvania would love to see this."

"Don't you worry, sweetie. You can get good pictures at the overlook up the road." Dymple patted her arm. "Are you vacationing in worm?"

Kate hesitated. She'd prepared herself to answer questions about her schooling and past employment without mentioning prison but hadn't expected this one. "It feels like a vacation, because I'm finally out of college. But I came to Wy-o-ming to do a marketing internship at the Whispering Pines Guest Ranch. They're going to train me this week for their tourist season, which starts next weekend, Memorial Day weekend."

If Dymple caught the Wyoming emphasis, she gave no indication. "Good for you. The Duncans are wonderful people and their ranch has an excellent reputation. A bright young lady like you will fit right in."

Kate wrinkled her nose. Maybe, except for the reputation part—and the bright part. She'd done so many stupid things, like trying to steal from yet another church. "So you know the owners?"

Dymple slid her hands in the pockets of her denim jumper. "Laura is a dear friend, and her son ..." Her eyes sparkled. "Michael is a remarkable young man, my adopted grandson. You'll like him."

"Wow, small world. You even know my new employer."

Dymple shrugged. "This is a typical small community, Kate. Everyone knows everybody in our little corner of the world—and everything they do."

Kate stifled a groan. She should have stayed in Pittsburgh, where she was just another face in the crowd.

Dymple tilted her head. "You're a long way from home. Why Wyoming?"

Kate stared into the woman's transparent eyes. She'd come west to distance herself from her past. But that was a secret nobody, not even a kindly little old lady named Dymple, could ever pry out of her. "Oh, I just wanted a change of scenery when I finished school."

"You made a good choice, Kate. Welcome to Wyoming." She motioned toward the chapel. "Feel free to stop any time. The Sunday service begins in about an hour. I think you'd like Pastor Chuck."

A bug crawled toward Kate's fingers on the railing. She brushed it away. Not that the pastor would like her. She wasn't ecclesiastical, the first word she'd learned in English

101 after Professor Eldridge challenged her online prison class to learn a new word every day. Over time, she'd become comfortable with multi-syllable words and with attending church services on the inside. But she wasn't good enough to attend church with regular people, people who hadn't done all the bad things she'd done. "Thanks, but I'd better not stay. I need to get to the ranch. The internship starts tomorrow morning."

"Vaya con Dios, Miss Kate."

Kate cocked her head.

"That's how my Mexican neighbors in California said goodbye. In English, it means go with God. Isn't that beautiful?"

"Yes, but I'm not sure God wants to go with me." Embarrassed by her confession, Kate turned to leave.

Dymple grasped her arm. "What did you mean by that comment?"

"Nothing, really." Kate chafed against Dymple's grasp, but the older woman held tight. She looked down. "I've done a lot of dumb things. I know God supposedly loves me and all that, but..."

Dymple released Kate's arm to gently lift her chin. "God not only loves you, sweetie, he delights in you."

Kate pulled back. "Delights?"

"Yes, Zephaniah—he wrote a book in the Bible—said God delights in you and sings about you."

"That'll be the day."

"He's singing right now. Your ears just aren't tuned to his frequency."

14

"I'll have to think about that." Kate looked at her watch. "I'd better get going. Thanks for the tour."

"You're welcome. I'll keep you in my prunes."

"Prunes?"

"Oh, dear." Dymple's crinkled cheeks turned pink. "I'm jumbling all my words today. Prayers. I'll keep you in my prayers." She waved her hand toward the cemetery. "Come see me again. I live on the other side, just beyond those trees."

"I'll do that." Kate started for the parking lot.

"One more thing," called her new friend. "Live your dream, Kate Neilson. Every day."

Indefatigable. Kate smiled, pleased to remember another word from English 101. She didn't know much about Dymple Forbes, but the petite lady appeared to be a woman of boundless energy.

She swiveled to tread the path back to the chapel. If only half the people she met in Wyoming were as interesting as...

She slowed, nearly stopping. What was that strange look on Dymple Forbes's face when they were talking in the cemetery? *Like she recognized me.*

But that was impossible. Her arrests had caught the local media's attention more than once, but surely Dymple didn't get Pittsburgh news out here in the middle of nowhere.

15

beckylyles.com

Made in the USA
Columbia, SC
03 July 2019